AN ELEPHANTASY

MARÍA ELENA WALSH

Translated by Daniel Hahn • Illustrated by Aurora Cacciapuoti

PUSHKIN CHILDREN'S BOOKS

Pushkin Children's Books
71–75 Shelton Street
London WC2H 9JQ

This translation of *An Elephantasy* was first published by Pushkin Press in 2016

Originally published in Spanish as *Dailan Kifki* in 1966

© Heiress to María Elena Walsh
c/o Schavelzon Graham Agencia Literaria
www.schavelzongraham.com

English Translation © Daniel Hahn 2016

Illustrations © Aurora Cacciapuoti 2016

10 9 8 7 6 5 4 3 2 1

ISBN 978 1 782690 99 3

Text designed and typeset by Tetragon, London

Proudly printed and bound in Great Britain by TJ International, Padstow, Cornwall

www.pushkinpress.com

I

O n Thursday, I went out nice and early to take my geranium for a little walk, like I did every Thursday. But no sooner had I opened the door, than... *Ker-BLAM!* What did I see? The front step was filled by a huge grey mountain blocking my way.

So what did I do? I pushed it! Yes, I pushed the mountain and managed to get it down onto the sidewalk. And there I saw—I was sure I had to be dreaming—that the mountain was nothing less than an elephant. Would you believe it? An elephant!

Well, I was about to scream for help when I noticed that the huge animal had a very large letter hanging from one of its ears. Someone had written my name in really big writing on the envelope. So I opened it, and this was what it said. Listen up:

> *Dear Miss,*
> *My name is Dailan Kifki, and I beg you not to be alarmed at the fact that I'm an elephant. My owner abandoned me because he is no longer able to feed me. He is sure that you, miss, with your good heart, would want to take care of me and cook me my yummy, lovely oats soup. I'm very hardworking and affectionate, and as for TV, I'm absolutely crazy about cartoons.*

Just imagine!

(Have you imagined?)

Well, you can guess what a problem this caused!

You might find a cat abandoned at your front door. You might find a dog, a cockroach, a stray ant... Even a baby in a nappy with a safety pin. Anything but an elephant!

It wouldn't have felt right just leaving him there like that, all abandoned and hungry. But on the other hand, even though we do have a big house, I really didn't know where to put him, and I had no idea what my family or our neighbours would say.

All the same, I decided to take him in just for a few days until we could find him someplace better.

You'd have done the same, right?

So I went back to pushing him, this time with his trunk facing indoors, his back end to the pavement, and without his offering the least resistance. He got himself inside very quickly, no doubt lured by the smell of rice pudding coming from the kitchen.

I took Dailan Kifki into the garden as stealthily as I could, trying not to wake anyone. But his footsteps boomed around the house like thunder, and soon my whole family appeared in their nightgowns at the window that looks out over the garden.

My mum fainted, my dad's pipe fell out of his mouth, and my brother Roberto said:

"We're toast."

Dailan Kifki just stood there in the garden, nice and calm, looking around casually and sniffing the flowers.

I went back inside to deal with my family, and on my way ordered four hundred thousand kilos of oats from the market, and fifty-four thousand, six-hundred-and-seventy-two dozen bananas, an army of bottles of milk and three croissants, all for my new houseguest.

When I got back to the garden, there was another surprise awaiting me.

What do you think Dailan Kifki was doing?

He was working!

Yes, you heard me right: working!

He was turning on the tap with his trunk, filling the watering can and then watering the plants, ever so delicately. As he walked, his big feet squashed flat all the ants he met along the way.

I could see then that what the letter had said was true: Dailan Kifki really was an extremely hardworking elephant.

There could surely be no other elephant like him in the world!

I was standing there watching him, full of admiration, when my Auntie Clodomira decided to show up at the house for a visit, with her umbrella and her hat that was covered in daisies.

When Auntie Clodomira saw Dailan Kifki in the garden, she fainted.

I was just about to call the fire brigade because my aunt is really fat and I couldn't get her out of the large plant pot she'd fallen into, when...

What do you think the elephant did?

He picked her up gently with his trunk, raised her through the bedroom window and set her down on the bed.

Then—still through the window—he fanned her with his ears, and stroked her softly.

As you can imagine, when my aunt woke up and saw she had an elephant as her nurse, she gave a terrible shriek and fainted again. But this didn't alarm Dailan Kifki.

Do you know what he did then?

He walked over to the kitchen, opened the fridge, took out a jug of cold water, pushed the door closed with his little foot, and then tipped the jug delicately over Auntie Clodomira's hat.

My family, meanwhile, were furious, and spurred on by my aunt's terrible cries, they all begged me tearfully to get *that monster* out of the house.

They screamed so much, I learnt later, that the uproar made all the stamps come unstuck from the post.

I had no choice but to say to Dailan Kifki:

"Come on, then, sweetheart, you'd better come with me. Nobody here understands you. Let's go. I'll take you to the zoo."

And what do you think Dailan Kifki answered?

Nothing. He started to cry, first two teeny little teardrops, then two great big teardrops, after that two absolutely huge teardrops and finally two hosepipe streams of tears.

He cried so loud that he made the whole block tremble and, naturally, the few stamps that were still stuck on the post came unstuck and flew out the windows.

My family were touched by this sorry sight, and had no choice but to stop their own crying. Everyone began trying to console him. Because the truth is, an elephant's sadness is much greater than a person's.

My father gave him a cookie, my Auntie Clodomira lent him her hat just for a little while, my mother stroked his ears and my brother Roberto said:

"We're toast."

And from that day on, Dailan Kifki lived in our garden.

2

I became very fond of Dailan Kifki. Which was why one night, when I heard him crying very softly, the sound just broke my heart.

Why would poor Dailan Kifki be crying, at midnight, in the garden?

Since his crying was becoming weepier and weepier, I was afraid that my family and our neighbours would wake up, or that the crying would be heard in the post office a second time and all the stamps would unstick themselves again. And so I got up, and just as I was, in my nightie, I put on my tulle hat with little flags and went out into the garden.

Dailan Kifki was crying like four elephants who had spent four whole years peeling onions.

"What's the matter, sweetheart?" I asked, gently.

"Oooohooooo!" he answered.

"What's up? Do you miss your mummy? Have you been bitten by a mosquito? Did you have a bad dream that a mouse was running after you?"

"No," he told me with a shake of his head, left-right, left-right.

And he took my hand with his trunk and placed it on his tummy.

I understood everything: the poor thing must have a tummy ache. It had to be indigestion from the forty-five buckets of rice pudding with cinnamon he'd eaten that day.

What a catastrophe!

If somebody like you, with your tiny tummy, knows how much your tummy hurts when it hurts, just imagine how much more an elephant's big belly would hurt, being so very huge.

I massaged it a bit, but this didn't seem to make it any better, so I decided to call the vet at once.

Still half asleep, I found the number in the phonebook and called, but the vet must have been asleep, and it was one of his patients who answered, because when I asked "Is that the vet speaking?" a grumpy voice replied "Woof!"

I phoned again, and another voice, just as grumpy, answered: "Meow!" So I didn't insist. In desperation, all I could think of was to call the fire brigade.

No sooner had I hung up the phone than a delightful Fireman appeared, all dressed in red, with a golden helmet with a plume, a hose with polka-dots and an axe that shone as bright as the moon.

"Where's the fire, where's the flame, that hides each time I call its name?" asked the Fireman.

"Look, Mr Fireman," I answered, "to tell you the truth, I can't actually offer you a fire just now, but..."

"But if there's no fire in forest or glade, no rescues to be most heroically made, then why did you call out the fire brigade?" he said.

"Let me explain, Mr Fireman. What happened is, Dailan Kifki has a tummy ache..."

"A fireman can't tell you how to fix an achy tummy. For such things, miss, I rather think you'd better ask your mummy."

"Firemen know about *everything*... And also, the vet was asleep. I got horrible answers like *woof* and *meow* when I called him, so please understand, Mr Fireman..."

"Very well, miss. For your sake, I will attend to this tummy ache," the Fireman answered, resigned.

I took him out to the garden without switching on the garden light so he wouldn't see, just like that, all of a sudden, that his patient was an elephant.

It was very dark in the garden, so when the Fireman heard a strange booming voice saying "Oooohooooo!" he was so startled that he grabbed me by the neck and jumped into my arms, and I had to pick him up like a little boy while he trembled and screamed "Mummy!"

What a spectacle.

"You should be ashamed," I said. "Fancy a fireman being scared!"

Then he recovered his cool, hopped back down to the ground, straightened his jacket, polished up his buttons with his sleeve and, grabbing hold of his axe and hose, headed towards Dailan Kifki.

"But what's this?" he cried. "It's an unearthly beast! It's a fiend from the east! A fearsome damsel-slayer, or a giant Himalaya?"

Then I turned on the light.

When he saw that his patient was an elephant, the Fireman sat down with a bump on his polka-dot hose.

With some effort I got him back up onto his feet. Impatiently now, I scolded him:

"Yessir, an elephant, that's right—so *why* did you get such a fright?"

"Very well, now, don't get irate. Don't get in a state. Don't yell at me, chide me, or grumble or prate," said the Fireman.

And he began to examine Dailan Kifki, who was crying more than ever now.

15

After examining him, the Fireman said:

"For elephant tummies, the best thing, it's true, is a soothing lettuce and sawdust brew."

So we went to the kitchen and got several heads of lettuce. But the sawdust was harder to find.

I thought about going round to wake up the Carpenter who lives on the corner, but the Fireman said:

"No, waking up a carpenter's a risky operation. His nightmares might pursue us and they lead to *devastation*."

So we made our way back into the house—quietly, so as not to wake my family—and we carried all the furniture out to the garden.

We grabbed hold of a saw and the two of us sawed chairs, tables, sideboards and shelves, until we had enough sawdust for a good dose of elephant medicine.

When we had managed to fill several buckets, the Fireman prepared the poultice of lettuce and sawdust, spread it out on a sheet and put it on Dailan Kifki's little tummy.

And we sat and waited for it to get better, while I brewed up some *mate* tea for the poor Fireman, who was exhausted and terribly sleepy.

We'd only had about seven hundred and forty-two *mate* teas each, and dawn had just begun to break, when at last Dailan Kifki stopped whimpering. He sighed, smiled and said, "Aaaah...", very relieved.

"Are you better now, kid?" we asked him.

Dailan Kifki told us yes, moving his big head up and down, up-down and down-up.

We covered the elephant well, sang him a lullaby duet, and finally Dailan Kifki fell very happily asleep.

I thanked the Fireman and gave him a little kiss. He trotted off in his red jacket, his golden helmet slightly askew, with his polka-dot hose and his axe that shone as bright as the moon.

And I went off to sleep, happy at having cured the terrible illness of my poor little elly with a sore little belly.

3

My father, my mother and my brother Roberto woke up, and straight away they all started crying and stamping their feet.

"What's going on?" I asked, absolutely exhausted after a bad night because of my sick elephant.

"What do you mean, what's going on?" asked my mum. "Can't you see I'm sitting in the air?"

I opened my eyes wide and went over to look.

It was true: Mum was sitting in the air because there wasn't a chair for her to sit on.

"And what about me?" shouted Dad. "Making me sleep standing in a corner! You think that's a nice way to behave?"

Just so: Dad was sleeping standing up because there was no longer a bed.

And my brother Roberto said:

"We're toast."

Which was quite right, since he, too, was sitting in the air opposite a cup of *café au lait* that was hanging from the light fitting because the poor thing had been left without a table.

And when they leant out the window to the garden, still in their nightgowns, they saw the remains of the furniture that the Fireman and I had sawn up so valiantly in the night, and they all screamed even louder than before.

They complained, they scolded me, my father promised to give me a good smacking on my backside and my brother Roberto said:

"We're toast—so very, very much toast," pointing at Dailan Kifki with an accusing finger.

What was worse, they sent me off to the carpenter's to order some new furniture.

"I can't spend the rest of my life sitting in the air, you know," complained my mother, quite correctly.

I ran off to the carpenter's on my own. Even though he was dying to tag along, I didn't want to take my elephant with me, as it would have overexcited the neighbours.

I knocked really loudly and the carpenter appeared, with his delightful wood-shaving beard that reached all the way down to his bellybutton.

"Good morning, Mister Carpenter," I said. "I've come to see whether you might have time this afternoon to make several pieces of furniture for my family."

"Are you totally mad?" he answered.

"No, I'm not, Mister Carpenter. I'll pay you double if necessary."

"Hm," said the carpenter, "and what about the wood, eh?"

"Well," I answered, "I would have thought that, being a good carpenter, you'd have wood, and nails, and a saw, and everything else you need, right?"

"Hm," he said again. "There's no wood."

"You're kidding. There's no wood?"

"None."

The carpenter moved towards me with a mysterious expression on his face, till he was so close his beard prickled at my ear, and he said:

"You know where you get wood from?"

"Of course," I answered. "From trees."

"Hm, and where are the trees?"

"Everywhere. In the forests, on the streets, in—"

"Hm... But if you cut trees down without permission, an officer will show up and... *smack.*"

That did alarm me, because I'd had more than enough threats of getting a smack at my own house.

"So what do we do now, Mister Carpenter?" I asked him desperately. "Where are we going to get the wood from?"

He didn't answer, but with an enigmatic gesture led me to his workshop, walking along a carpet of shavings, sawdust and sweetly scented woodblocks. He lit a lamp, lifted up a floorboard, and pulled out a chest.

Inside the chest there was a box.

Inside the box there was another box.

Inside that box there was another box.

Inside that box there was a briefcase.

Inside the briefcase there was a small bag.

Inside the small bag there was a velvet case.

Inside the velvet case there was a purse.

Inside the purse there was a little packet wrapped up in tissue paper.

Inside the little packet wrapped up in tissue paper there was a bean.

The carpenter gave it a quick polish with his sleeve and held it out to me.

"And what am I supposed to do with this bean, Mister Carpenter?" I asked, sure he'd gone quite mad.

"What are you supposed to do? You plant it, of course!"

"Plant it? What for, if I might know?"

"What for? From the bean will come a shoot and from the shoot a twig, from a branch will come a trunk and from the trunk a whole tree and way up there, way up on top, the birdies will be singing."

"But Mister Carpenter," I said, distressed, "when the tree has grown and there are birdies singing on top, we'll be very sorry to have to cut it down to make wood. And besides, Mum will be fed up of sitting in the air by then."

"Well, what can you do?" said the carpenter. "If you want wood, plant the bean."

And he shut the door in my face! I walked away, so very sad, with the bean in my hand, seeing that I had no choice but to plant it and wait for it to grow.

When I got home, my family bombarded me with questions.

"Hang on," I answered. "Have a bit of patience. You don't just make furniture overnight, you know. Wait a little..."

And I went off to the garden to plant my bean, while they all sat there in the air in a filthy mood.

Dailan Kifki helped me plant it, treading down the earth with his big steamroller feet.

Once the bean was nicely sown, we sat down on the grass to wait for it to grow.

I pretended not to be paying attention and didn't look at it much, because I knew that if you looked at it, it would take longer to grow, in the same way a pot of milk takes longer to boil.

But a good long while went by... and nothing.

Then two whiles went by... and still nothing.

Then a really, really *big* while went by... and still nothing.

The bean didn't even give out the tiniest, rubbishest shoot.

Without wasting another moment, and certain that the carpenter must have swindled me, I went round to his place and dragged him back with me by his delightful, celestial, wood-shaving beard.

The carpenter dug up the bean and said:

"Hm... Well, quite!"

"Quite what? Didn't we plant it right?"

"You planted it the wrong way round! Can't you see it's growing downward?"

And we saw that the bean was, indeed, the wrong way round. It had sprouted a long green beard, but pointing downward.

The carpenter planted it the right way up, Dailan Kifki once again trod down the earth with one of his big feet, and I instructed him to keep an eye on it for a little while.

Then I went to explain to my mum that, as it turned out, getting hold of wood to make furniture wasn't as simple as it first appeared.

My mum was still sitting in the air.

Poor Mum.

4

That afternoon, when I got back from work, I found a big crowd of people outside my house.

Whatever could have happened? I thought in alarm.

I could hear policemen's whistles, ambulance sirens, the tinkling triangles of the wafer sellers, people screaming and sighing and shouting and having tantrums.

I shoved my way through as best I could.

Everybody was yelling and arguing, looking up towards the sky. The police officers were trying to keep order.

There were photographers and reporters, a TV news team, a dog with two tails, firemen eating meringues and children who were just there taking advantage of the commotion to skip some school.

"What's going on?" I asked, still alarmed.

Nobody answered. Some of them because they didn't feel like it. Others because they were too busy eating ice creams. Others because they didn't know what was going on either.

Since everybody was looking up, over the back of my house, I looked up too. And what do you think I saw? Only Dailan Kifki asleep on the tall, super-tall trunk of a tall, super-tall tree! So tall it seemed to be feather-dusting the clouds with its leaves.

"It can't be," I said to myself. "I must be dreaming... How did Dailan Kifki manage to climb up there?"

"Isn't it an outrage?" remarked one of our neighbours. "When have you ever seen an elephant on top of a tree, eh? And what if it falls? What if it squashes someone flat? The government should *not* be allowing elephants to climb trees!"

"Yes, you're quite right, ma'am," I answered, choosing not to point out that the elephant was my elephant and that his name was Dailan Kifki.

I kept on pushing my way through and saying lots of excuse-mes until I managed to get into my house, which was also full of people, security guards, firemen, cameramen, dogs, cats, ice-cream sellers, balloon sellers and even a nun who was saying prayers to calm everyone down.

My mother threw her arms around me, crying, and said:

"You see what a disaster it is? I told you it would have been best to take that elephant to the zoo!"

"But Mum, where did Dailan Kifki find such a tall tree?"

"That tree is your famous bean!" said Mum between sobs.

"My bean? It's grown that much?" I asked.

And my mother told me the whole story.

After planting the bean, I left Dailan Kifki in charge of looking after it.

It seems the poor thing had fallen asleep... right on top of where the bean was planted.

And of course, the bean began to grow at full speed... Just think of the effort that poor little bean must have made lifting an elephant! Can you imagine? Well, the fact is that the little plant grew, and it grew, and it grew... It started sprouting little twigs, then branches, then tree-trunks... And of course, on the way it picked up poor Dailan Kifki, who really is a very deep sleeper.

The fact was, the bean had been transformed into a lovely tree, at whose summit a sleeping elephant was rocking gently.

I made the crowds quiet down because I was afraid they would wake him up and he'd fall. And I started thinking very anxiously about what we could do to get him safely back to earth.

My mother was still complaining:

"But doesn't this elephant understand we need the tree to make the wood to make the furniture?"

I asked her to have a little patience, as there was absolutely no way we could chop the tree down and give poor innocent Dailan Kifki such a terrible bump.

I came up with various ideas for getting him down safely.

The first was to ask a helicopter to approach him slowly. But I immediately thought the roaring noise would startle him.

I also thought about asking the firemen for their ladder. But how was the poor thing, with his great big feet, supposed to come down such flimsy steps?

Impossible.

At that point my brother Roberto arrived, looked up and said: "We're toast."

Then it occurred to him that the best plan would be to soap the tree-trunk so that Dailan Kifki would just slide down. But I didn't think that was such a good idea.

Then my dad, who's a practical man, suggested that someone ought to climb the tree and tie a cable from the top of the tree to the top of a nearby skyscraper, that we should give Dailan Kifki a little parasol and that he would then walk across like a tightrope-walker till he'd arrived safe and sound on top of the skyscraper.

"Yes, Dad, it's an excellent plan," I said. "But you haven't thought about the next problem we'd have. When Dailan Kifki arrives on top of the skyscraper, how do we get him down then? He won't fit in a lift, and he doesn't know how to go down stairs."

Dad had no answer for this, and only managed to scratch a little behind his ear. Then my Auntie Clodomira showed up twirling her umbrella and said:

"See? I told you that elephant was going to cause you a headache. Such an impudent creature. Isn't the big beast ashamed to be perched up there like he's some kind of bird?"

"Please, Auntie," I replied, "now isn't the moment for a telling-off. The most urgent thing is for us to get him down from the tree without him hurting himself."

"Oh, but that's the easiest thing in the world!" said my aunt.

"You think so, Auntie? What should we do?"

"You have to bend the trunk of the tree down, nice and slowly, bit by bit..."

"And what if it breaks?" I asked.

"Well, I hadn't thought of that," replied my Auntie Clodomira. And she immediately forgot all about the problem and started dictating a recipe to my mother for cork sponge with candied spinach.

Then my brother Roberto, who by now was quite furious at so much commotion, could only say:

"I'll get that elephant down with my slingshot!"

I nearly hit him then, but I stopped myself because I was worried the noise of the thwack would wake Dailan Kifki.

Meanwhile, I looked up again and saw that Dailan Kifki was stretching. He woke up gently, like an angel. Everybody watched him, mouths agape, while the photographers took his picture and the cameramen filmed him.

When he had woken up he seemed quite astonished, because he stared down with a look of utter wonderment.

Luckily he didn't fall as he's a clever elephant and he'd realised that, strange as it seemed, he had fallen asleep on top of a tree.

Seeing him wide awake, I took the opportunity to give him a good scolding.

"Oh, that's just lovely, Dailan Kifki," I shouted, "just lovely! So, what, you think you're a little birdie, then?"

And do you know what the cheeky fellow replied?

Mocking me, with his big booming voice, he replied:

"*CHEEP CHEEP CHIRRUP CHEEP!*"

I wasn't expecting that.

5

Well then, as I was saying, there we were with cricks in our necks from all the hours we'd spent looking up at Dailan Kifki, and still nobody had thought of a truly effective method for getting him down from the tree. To tell you the truth, since he liked it and he felt like a little birdie—which was completely unforgivable, according to my aunt—we could really have left him there and just sent food up to him somehow, except that we urgently needed to chop down the tree to get wood to make the furniture for my house. So there wasn't a minute to lose.

I made a decision: I'd go fetch the Fireman. Who else would be better at thinking up clever ideas for getting Dailan Kifki down from the tree? No one, that's who.

So I telephoned the Fireman, and before I'd even finished hanging up, there he was, in his lovely red jacket, his golden helmet with a plume, his polka-dot hose and his axe that shone as bright as the moon.

"What should we do, Mister Fireman?" I asked him, most distressed. And the Fireman replied, very serious:

"For hunting down an elephant who thinks he is a bird, there's only one solution—just you wait—I'll say the word..."

"Very well, Mister Fireman. Tell me your method."

And the Fireman whispered, very secretly, in my ear.

When he had explained it properly, I almost fainted in wonder at such a clever fireman.

I put on my tulle hat with little flags and ran out to the street, which was still full of people nibbling on caramels and unwrapping lollipops.

I went straight over to the supermarket. I bought seven hundred and eighty dozen balls of thick twine, upholstery needles, tissue paper, paste, six hundred and seventy-eight kilometres of tulle in all kinds of colours, hat feathers, wooden rods, cellophane, silk ribbons and a kilo and a half of some thing or other I don't remember now.

I took it all home, and in the garden the Fireman and I set to work, while everyone watched us in amazement and my brother Roberto just kept on repeating again and again like a parrot:

"We're toast, we're toast, we're toast."

Oh, how the Fireman and I worked!

For hours we sewed, glued, unglued, trimmed, darned and knotted, we did and undid, because the Fireman never felt the job was quite perfect.

Fortunately Mum felt sorry for us and brewed us some *mate* tea.

Every once in a while I would look up just to check how Dailan Kifki was doing.

"How are you doing, sweetheart?" I shouted.

"*CHIRRUP CHEEP,*" he replied.

W hen our work was finally ready, it was nearly dark.

And it was time to tell everybody what it was the Fireman and I had been making. A pair of wings!

A lovely pair of wings so that Dailan Kifki could fly down and land in the garden safe and sound.

See how clever the Fireman was?

And to think it hadn't occurred to anyone else!

Those wings were very beautiful. Just picture them: tulle in all kinds of colours, with little feathers, cellophane trimmings, finished with silver paper, silk ribbons, and even a rosette the Fireman added at the last minute.

The most difficult job was still to come: climbing up the tree and putting the wings on Dailan Kifki. But the Fireman said bravely:

"Adorning Mister Elephant with such a pair of wings? It's nothing too alarming, quite the easiest of things."

As the Fireman was getting ready to climb the tree, my whole family came out to the garden to see him off, as though he were going to China or to Mars on a rocket.

My mother hugged him, sobbing, and gave him a noisy kiss.

My father clapped him on the back and said:

"Be brave, my friend."

My Auntie Clodomira, at the very last moment, sewed a button onto his jacket, and my brother Roberto simply said:

"We're toast."

While we all waved our handkerchiefs at him and shouted encouragement, the Fireman started to climb the tree. It was difficult since he was loaded up with those wings, which were huge.

Fortunately, at that moment the Boy Scouts' band showed up and set about playing a march that really helped to raise the Fireman's spirits.

In the final stretch, when it was beginning to look like he was going to fall, defeated by the weight of the wings, and all twitchy because a butterfly had just settled on his nose, Dailan Kifki gave him a little help, picking him up with his trunk and setting him down beside him on top of the tree.

The Fireman got to his feet, struck his breast valiantly, let out a great yell like Tarzan and grandly flourished his golden helmet with a plume.

The hard part was over.

6

When she saw him at the top of the tree, my mum said:

"What a brave fireman. You ought to marry that one, my girl."

Which embarrassed me terribly, as you can imagine.

I ran to fetch my spyglass to get a better view of what the Fireman was doing all the way up there.

I could see that he had climbed onto Dailan Kifki's head and was putting on the elephant's wings.

Dailan Kifki seemed to be finding it ticklish, because he was giggling and shaking all over. He was bucking about so much I was scared he'd make the Fireman fall.

So my family, just as a precaution, brought all the mattresses, pillows and cushions out into the garden and arranged them around the tree, so as to soften any dangerous bump that might occur.

"I ought to have lent him my umbrella," said Auntie Clodomira.

"What for, Auntie? It's not raining," I said, beginning to get rather annoyed with her.

"To use as a parachute in case of emergency," replied my aunt.

I must say, those wings did look lovely on Dailan Kifki.

By the light of the sun's last rays, you can't imagine how those cellophane trims, the ribbons and the rosette all shone!

Fortunately the wind picked up a little, which apart from being helpful for flying also made the tulle of his wings flutter.

When the Fireman was sure the wings were firmly affixed, he waved us goodbye with his arm raised high in the air, flourished his helmet with a plume, settled himself comfortably on the elephant's head, and spurred him on with his heels. Then Dailan Kifki unfurled his wings and... *Zzzzzzooooom!* away he flew.

We all clapped frantically, while the Fireman waved and Dailan Kifki, just fooling around, did two or three pirouettes in the air.

We were so excited at the success of our undertaking that at first we didn't notice that this new spaceship, rather than coming straight down into the garden, was off through the air, flying faster and faster and higher...

"But where are they going?" I asked, slightly alarmed.

"Did you advise the Fireman to land right away?" asked my dad.

"No," I answered. "A fireman doesn't need anyone giving him instructions. He always knows exactly what to do."

"But what if he doesn't come back? How are you going to marry him then?" asked my mum with a pout, her bottom lip starting to quiver.

"We need to bring them down with a slingshot," said my brother Roberto softly, as he looked—green with envy—at the astronautical Fireman.

We stood there dumbstruck, watching as Dailan Kifki fluttered high above our house.

He seemed to have no intention whatsoever of coming down to land.

I have to admit, I was jealous, too, just like my brother Roberto.

Can you imagine how beautiful it would be to glide through the air on a flying elephant?

"Why didn't you go up with him?" asked my mother.

"It didn't occur to me," I replied, "which is a shame. Look at the journey I've missed! They'll probably get up to the moon and everything..."

Then my mum started waving at the Fireman with a hankie, gesturing for him to come down. But the Fireman didn't understand her. He thought she was waving a hello and just waved back, with exaggerated flourishes of his golden helmet.

He did so many waves and bows he almost fell off the elephant. Dailan Kifki had to straighten him up again with a rather energetic whack of his trunk.

They climbed higher and higher. By the time we'd realised it, they were out of sight. And night had fallen.

My brother Roberto said:

"We're toast."

This time I had to agree.

7

That night we had a family meeting, all of us sitting on the floor like Native Americans because, as you'll remember, we'd been left without any furniture.

My mum said:

"We have to report Dailan Kifki's escape to the police."

My dad said:

"No, this is a matter for the local council."

According to my Auntie Clodomira:

"No, we need to inform the UFO investigation centre."

And my brother Roberto said:

"We're toast."

"Meanwhile," I said, my own bottom lip starting to quiver now, "poor Dailan Kifki is flying around the sky with nobody to make him his lovely oats soup."

Then suddenly we heard three loud knocks on the front door.

Knock,
    and *Knock*
        and *Knock.*

I leapt up:

"It's them, they're back!"

I ran over to open the door, and who do you think I found?

Dailan?

No.

The Fireman?

No.

I found a different fireman. A huge one with moustaches like motorcycle handlebars, his jacket covered in insignias, medals, stripes, epaulettes, braid and rosettes.

The Big Fireman saluted and introduced himself:

"I'm Captain of the Fireman crew. *Hurroo hurroo hurray!*"

I saluted back, and with some alarm I asked him what he wanted. He replied, solemnly:

"One fireman's missing—what to do? He's not been seen all day!"

"A fireman?" I said, acting all absent-minded. "What fireman?"

"I counted them at breakfast time, and one had gone astray!"

"Oh... Yes, Mister Captain," I answered, blushing. "Yes, it's quite true, there was a fireman here, but, um... But I think he's just popped out for a bit."

The Captain insisted:

"No, no, I'm sure as sure can be, you've hidden him away!"

I let him in so he could search the house. As my family watched in astonishment, the Captain looked inside the fridge, behind the flowerpots and under the rug.

Naturally, he found no trace of the Fireman. Then the Captain frowned at me, and said:

"Put on your hat and come with me, our tram ride will be brief—we're off to the Police HQ, 'cos you're a fireman thief!"

Can you imagine such an outrage? Me, arrested? Me, a thief!

I wanted to protest, but he was staring so hard at me that I put on my hat without a word, said goodbye to my family and left with the Captain. Once we were out on the street, he took me by the hand and walked me to the bus stop.

We finally reached the police station, where we were seen by a blue superintendent. Fortunately he was very nice indeed, because I was trembling with fear.

Well, the Captain made his accusation, pointing at me and telling the Superintendent that I'd stolen a fireman.

"That's just not true, Mister Superintendent," I protested.

And we began to argue, all three of us at once. Or, rather, I should say the four of us, because there was someone else there.

A parrot. The Superintendent's parrot who, to make matters worse, only knew how to say:

"We're-toast-we're-toast-we're-toast-we're-toast."

As if I really needed to hear those words.

Meanwhile the Captain took a little hankie out of his cuff and wept like a lunatic for his lost fireman.

"Well then, miss," said the Superintendent. "You just return the Fireman and we'll say no more about it."

"But I haven't got him, Mister Superintendent. Didn't I tell you the Fireman just popped out for a bit?"

"Well then, tell me where he's popped out to and I'll send for him right away. My three guards can go fetch him."

And then I fell silent, because I was embarrassed to have to admit that the Fireman had popped out for a flight through the air on the back of an elephant.

Who would believe me?

No one, that's who.

But still I told them the truth, and sure enough, neither of them believed me. Nor did the parrot.

They started to laugh.

But I repeated the story to them so seriously that they ended up believing me.

Then the Superintendent said that, since a flying elephant could be a serious danger to the city, we would have to alert the local council at once.

And so the three of us took the bus over to the Town Hall. The parrot stayed behind to look after the police station, the three guards and the prisoner.

I was very pleased that they hadn't put me in prison, so on the way I bought an ice cream for the Captain and a balloon for the Superintendent.

We reached the Town Hall and were met by the secretary of the secretary of the secretary of the secretary of the secretary of the Mayor.

Many hours later we were received by the Mayor in person, who was wearing a lovely green frock coat, a cardboard top hat and an enormous tin watch on his tummy.

He greeted us in a very friendly manner and invited us to sit in three little gold chairs.

We told him the whole story, and the Mayor looked very surprised and distressed. Then he called for a huge map of THE CITY OF BUENOS AIRES and told me to point to the area where Dailan Kifki and the Fireman might be flying round about now.

"I don't know, Mister Mayor," I replied. "Around here... or rather, maybe a bit more like that way?"

I took my finger off the map and just pointed up at the sky.

"Hm," said the Mayor, thoughtfully. "If you think they're still in the sky and haven't come down yet onto some street, or park, or small square or public boulevard or building or avenue of Buenos Aires, we will have to refer the matter to the Ministry of Aeronautics, because this isn't a problem that we at the Town Hall will be able to solve."

So off we all went, the Captain, the Superintendent, the Mayor and me, to get the bus over to the Ministry of Aeronautics.

8

We arrived at the Ministry of Aeronautics and were greeted by the Mini-Secretary.

I had to tell the whole story all over again: that I had an elephant called Dailan Kifki who had flown away with the Fireman riding on his back.

The Mini-Secretary listened to the story in amazement, and said it was the first time such a deed had ever been accomplished in the whole country. He congratulated me for having such an intelligent elephant, he congratulated the Captain for having such a brave Fireman, and he was left with no choice but to congratulate the Superintendent for having such a green parrot. (The Superintendent's bottom lip had started to quiver because he wasn't being congratulated, too.)

The Mini-Secretary said the travellers were an honour to the land and advised the Mayor to put Dailan Kifki's name on some corner, or square, or public boulevard or lane in Buenos Aires.

"Well, then," said the Mini-Secretary, "I would have no trouble putting a helicopter at your disposal to fly around the sky looking for the fugitives, but since there's a chance they may have crossed the border and might now be flying in the skies over Chile or some other sister nation of ours, we would do best to alert the embassies of the bordering countries."

So to cut a long story short: within five minutes we were all on a bus headed for the embassies of Chile, Uruguay, Paraguay, Bolivia, Brazil and—just in case—Peru.

The Ambassadors seemed most interested in the case. They said that if Dailan Kifki and his pilot did happen to be flying in the skies above their respective countries, they would be returned to Argentina with all possible honours and without having to pay customs duties.

"Hang on just a moment," said one of the Ambassadors. "We've forgotten something very important!"

"What have we forgotten, Mister Ambassador?" I asked, slightly alarmed.

"What if they're flying over sea, what then? And what if they fall in the water?"

He was totally, completely right. There was a possibility that Dailan Kifki and the Fireman would fall into the sea—and they weren't wearing their swimming trunks or life-vests.

"That's right," said the Mini-Secretary of Aeronautics. "How did we not think of that? We have to take the bus right away to the Ministry of the Navy and ask them for lifeboats."

So off we all went—a whole retinue.

The Captain of the Firemen led the way, waving his axe, his hose wrapped around his body like a snake.

After him came the Mini-Secretary of Aeronautics, his arms spread wide like a plane, making an engine noise with his mouth.

Then came the Mayor twirling The Keys of Buenos Aires.

And then, in the following order—if I'm not mistaken—came...

The Brazilian ambassador, playing maracas and dancing a *samba*,

The Bolivian ambassador dancing the *carnavalito*,

The Uruguayan ambassador dancing the *candombe*,

The Paraguayan ambassador sucking on an orange and dancing the polka,

The Chilean ambassador tapping out a *cueca*,

The Peruvian ambassador singing a little *huayno* at the top of his lungs,

And finally me, awfully embarrassed at the thought that a simple elephant could cause such an outrage here on the street.

We reached the Ministry of the Navy and were met by a most Admirable Admiral, all in white, who looked like he'd just been bathing in milk, chalk and starch.

We explained the situation and he listened very attentively while smoking his pipe and covering us with soap bubbles.

The Admiral made calls on a lot of telephones, scratched his ear and finally, climbing up onto the desk, gave the following speech:

"Your excellencies Misters Ambassadors and other dignitaries here present: this Ministry has no trouble putting at your disposal a number of Navy units to work together towards the rescue of the travellers, but since the aforementioned travellers might have embarked on a journey into space, I would suggest that we first attempt to locate them via the Astronomical Observatory in La Plata."

I slumped down into a chair. I was beginning to lose hope, but I did have to acknowledge that the Admiral was correct.

We would have to look at the whole sky with a telescope to locate the travellers before going ahead with our plans.

The Admiral very kindly agreed to accompany us to the city of La Plata, and this time he was at the head of the retinue.

We all walked through the centre of town, drawing such attention to ourselves that many more people joined us, so that by the time we reached Constitución we looked more like the crowd pouring out of the Boca stadium after a Sunday game.

Using his whistle, his truncheon and his white gloves, the Superintendent managed to move the busybodies away, and finally we were able to board the train.

But just as it was about to pull out of the station, the Captain counted us and discovered someone was missing.

It was none other than the Mini-Secretary of Aeronautics, who was only little and had gone missing in the crowd.

The Captain ran off to fetch him and led him back by the ear. The train was already beginning to move off by the time they boarded.

But as it turned out, our misfortunes had barely begun...

9

At last we arrived at La Plata, and after stopping off for a nice hot chocolate with bread and butter and sugar to recover our strength, we went straight over to the Astronomical Observatory.

We were met by a very sweet little old man. We knew he had to be the Director because his lapels were covered in stardust and he had a little piece of comet's tail tangled in his wig.

Since he was a bit deaf, it took us three hours to make him understand that what we wanted was to look through the telescope for an elephant flying with a fireman on his back.

When he did finally understand, he fainted. We revived him with a peperina tea and a biscuit.

Calmer now, the old man said:

"As spaceships go, this UFO does sound very strange indeed. But since you're such important people, you may look through the telescope to your hearts' content."

So we looked. One by one. Taking strict turns.

And what did we see?

The first thing I saw was a star sitting comfortably in a wicker chair. Then I saw another, bigger star with a bow in the centre. Then I saw the moon, and I looked very closely to try to make out Dailan walking among the craters.

Suddenly I yelled:

"There they are, I've seen them! It's them! They're walking around on the moon!"

Everybody leapt at the telescope, but the Director moved them away and looked through it himself very carefully, before saying:

"No, miss, I'm sorry to tell you that what you're seeing is not an elephant walking around on the moon. It's a fly walking around on the lens of the telescope."

I was so disappointed I didn't want to look any more.

The little old Observatory Director looked again through several different telescopes, and said finally:

"I can see no trace of any astronautical elephant, but I might perhaps suggest one thing. It could be your last hope."

"What's that, Mister Director?" I asked.

And the Director replied wisely:

"It's possible that sooner or later Dailan Kifki's wings will get tangled in the tail of a kite."

"And if that happens, what can we do, Mister Director?" we all asked.

"I would be happy to accompany you to the Union of Kite-Flyers of the Argentine Republic."

We all marvelled at the Director's incredible wisdom. Without a moment to lose, off we went to the station to take the train back to the capital.

We thought of going straight to Ituzaingó, where the Union had its Headquarters, but it was getting late.

The Captain decided we had to wait till the following morning, because everyone knows that nobody ever flies a kite at night-time.

I was thinking: What should I do with all these people who've been so kind? I can't just leave them hanging around out there all night.

The Admiral suggested we go to his boat to do some manoeuvres.

The Mini-Secretary was adamant that we go for a ride in his plane.

The Captain wanted to camp out in Constitution Square, start a nice little fire and spend the night out in the open.

So I decided to invite them all round to my house.

Really, it was the least I could do.

10

So as I was saying, we all boarded the subway train back to my house.

You can imagine my family's surprise when I showed up so many hours later and in the company of so many important people!

My Auntie Clodomira gave each of them her hand, and then a short while later gave each of them her hand all over again, repeating delightedly:

"Pleasedtomeetyoupleasedtomeetyoupleasedtomeetyou- pleasedtomeetyou."

My brother Roberto said:

"We're toast."

Dad invited them all to take a seat in the air and ran to the kitchen to brew some *mate* for our guests.

Mum took me into a corner to talk in secret.

"Listen, my girl," she said, "we really must throw a party now, seeing as you've brought such jolly people with you."

"But Mum," I replied, "how are we going to have a party if we're all so sad?"

"Why are you sad?" asked my mum, who always has her head in the clouds.

"What do you mean, why? Can't you see we haven't been able to find Dailan Kifki, or the Fireman? Can't you see there's no trace of them at all, not in space or in the clouds or on the moon or in the stars? Can't you see that when it gets light we're going to have to go off, all over again, on our expedition?"

"It doesn't matter, they'll turn up," answered my mum. "The Fireman will turn up and then you can marry him. But in the meantime let's throw a party!"

And she took me into the kitchen to make sandwiches.

There wasn't enough food in my house for so many people, so we had to use a bit of the sawdust that was left over from Dailan Kifki's medicine and cut a few little ferns and geranium leaves to eat with the bread.

We served the sandwiches, while my Auntie Clodomira turned on the lights and started up the record-player.

We needed the guests to dance and get distracted so they wouldn't notice the lack of furniture.

So we all ate geranium sandwiches, we drank *mate*, orange squash and cold water and we danced the night away.

I should mention that, since it was a long night, there was a point at which the *mate* and the orange squash ran out, so my mother sent me off to prepare some tap water with watercolour paint. It really looked like orangeade, even if the taste wasn't exactly very nice.

At the height of the dancing I saw my Auntie Clodomira chatting excitedly in a corner with the Superintendent, and I wouldn't have been surprised to learn that by the next day or the following they were a couple.

The party was very lively, to the great outrage of the neighbours, who all showed up in their nightshirts and nightcaps carrying candles and saying, in unison:

"*Sssshhhhhhhhhhhh!*"

But when they discovered that it wasn't, in fact, a party but a pause in the middle of a dangerous expedition to rescue Dailan Kifki, they decided to stay, and then to go with us.

As if there weren't enough of us!

It was already getting light when the Superintendent stood right in the middle of the living room, stretched out his arms with white gloves at their ends and blew noisily on his whistle.

We all presumed he simply wanted to direct the dancing so we wouldn't all keep shoving into each other.

Nope.

"Halt!" he shouted. "It's time to get ready for our journey to Ituzaingó to make the necessary arrangements with the Union of Kite-Flyers."

"We're all coming, too," said Mum.

"No, Mum," I protested. "There are far too many of us already."

"Absolutely not," replied my mum. "Either we all go, or no one goes."

"Yes, that's right, we're coming!" said my dad.

And my brother Roberto added:

"We're toast."

The person who was most insistent on joining the retinue was my Auntie Clodomira, who was clinging tightly to the Superintendent's arm.

I could tell they weren't going to be dissuaded, because they're all very stubborn.

My mother packed the crumbs left over from the sawdust-and-geranium sandwiches into a hamper, and put on her hat.

My father put on his rubber boots and his little poncho.

My brother Roberto put on his sheriff's star.

And out we all went, hand in hand in hand, to take the bus to Miserere Square, where the train station was.

We were so very sleepy, and so exhausted from all the dancing, I'm sure we all looked quite drunk.

We all fell asleep on the bus. You can't imagine how loudly the Mayor snored, and how wonky my Auntie Clodomira's hat was!

The Conductor had to wake us with a shout:

"*Next stop: Miserere Squaaaaare!*"

The Mini-Secretary had fallen asleep in my mother's arms.

We all got off, terribly embarrassed, and ran to catch the train to Ituzaingó.

II

Of course, we fell asleep on the train, too, and when I woke up all of a sudden, I saw that we'd come to a stop at Moreno, the end of the line.

With a great deal of effort I managed to wake the others, shaking them and shouting in their ears, and with even more effort I managed to get them off the train to wait for another train to take us back to Ituzaingó.

On the journey from Moreno to Ituzaingó I put my fingers in my eyes *like this* to keep them open, because somebody had to stay awake so we wouldn't all just go right back to Miserere Square again, and from there back to Moreno, and from there to Miserere Square, and so on.

Once we'd reached Ituzaingó station, the Captain of the Firemen lined us all up, counted us off and, plugging his hose into a tap, gave us a good shower so we'd finish waking up.

We had all been planning to go straight to the Union of Kite-Flyers, but my mother cried:

"Just a moment, gentlemen!"

"What's going on, Mum?" I asked, in alarm.

"I've only just remembered," replied my mum. "Here in Ituzaingó is where your granddad lives—that is, my father. We should go fetch him so that he can come with us on our expedition."

"No, Mum. Please," I replied, "there are far too many of us already. Leave Granddad in peace."

But my mum said:

"No, no and no."

So we had no choice but to set out, all of us together hand in hand, for Granddad's house, which was thirty-five blocks from the station.

12

You don't know what my granddad's like, of course. He's a little old man with a beard and spectacles, very wise and scholarly, but a terrible grouch. I wasn't especially close to him, because he was always trying to make me go back to school. Actually, the truth is, he's always trying to make *everybody* go to school.

Which was why when we were at Ituzaingó station I'd been trying to persuade my mum that we shouldn't go fetch him.

Meanwhile, the people who were waiting for the train started looking at us as if we were the most peculiar creatures. When we set off towards Granddad's house, three newspaper salesmen attached themselves to our group, along with two guards, four tramps, a wafer seller and four altar boys who'd escaped from church.

At last we reached Granddad's house, all muddy, scratched by nettles and bitten by mosquitoes, because the house is at the back of beyond—"where the devil lost his poncho", as they say around here. The Superintendent even had to pick up my Auntie Clodomira to get her over a puddle...

Granddad was sleeping like a little cherub.

We tried waking him but it was quite impossible. He'd covered his head with a pillow and pulled his nightcap down over his ears.

My mum got him up and dressed, while Granddad, who was still half asleep, put up a fine grumbling and kicking.

When he was dressed and his face washed, he asked what all this upheaval was about, since today wasn't a school day and anyway this, that and the other.

We explained that we'd come to fetch him to join a glorious expedition, and then Granddad livened up at last.

He went over to a cobweb-covered trunk and took out an explorer's helmet, a pop-gun, a butterfly net, a compass, a cap-gun and a tin sword.

Thus equipped—and when it looked like he'd finally been convinced—Granddad, who's temperamental as the devil, sat down on the floor and said:

"No, I'm just not going. I don't want to."

So, to persuade him, I said:

"But Granddad, you have to come, so that when we find Dailan Kifki you can make the official speech!"

Since he absolutely loves making speeches, and he loves school overalls, blackboards, herbariums and all those kinds of things, he agreed enthusiastically, on condition that we sang the *San Lorenzo March* on the way. Which we did quite reluctantly, as we were hoarse from so much chattering, dancing, planning, bus-riding, train-riding, arguing, etc.

Finally, with Granddad at the head of the party, and singing the *San Lorenzo March*, we walked across puddles, over ditches, past wire fences and through marshes till we reached a farmhouse in the middle of wide open countryside, where a sign with several spelling mistakes read:

"UNION OF KITE-FLYERS"

At last!

13

We knocked on the door of the Union and a boy appeared. He was freckled and idle, and had clearly never washed his face in his life. And as for his knees—well, the less said, the better.

Granddad looked him up and down, and right then and there gave him a fierce telling-off. Then he grabbed him by the ear and made him stand facing the wall as punishment.

"But Granddad," I said, "you shouldn't be fighting with people from the Union because then they won't want to help us fish for Dailan Kifki and the Fireman."

It was no use.

Granddad just went right on scolding and threatening the poor boy, who was looking at all of us in complete amazement, as if we were wild beasts from a circus or a collection of museum animals.

Then I gently pulled Granddad aside and with a big smile said to the Union kid:

"Good morning, little boy!"

"What's with the 'little boy'!" he replied. "Have a bit more respect! I'm the Secretary of the Union of Kite-Flyers, don't you know?"

"Well then," I replied, alarmed at his cheek and lack of manners, "well then, Mister Secretary, we've come to ask you a big favour."

"We want you to wash your face and learn to spell!" roared Granddad.

And the Superintendent had to shut him up by waving his truncheon and giving a long blow on his whistle.

"What the devil do you want from us at this time of day?" asked the Secretary of the Union, most rudely. (I hope he's not a friend of yours.)

Then I told him the whole story: that my elephant Dailan Kifki had flown off with a fireman riding on his back, and that we wanted to find out whether he had become tangled in the tail of some kite.

"Whoah..." was all the boy said, his mouth open and a finger to his temple as though I were barmy.

"But it's true!" I protested. "Why else do you think so many important people have come here, all of them exhausted and bitten by mosquitoes, if we aren't dealing with a truly catastrophic and abominable calamity?"

But the rude child, who was ready to close the door in our faces, just replied:

"All this trouble for one good-for-nothing elephant!"

"Actually this is a very serious matter..." I said, my bottom lip about to quiver again.

"What do I care?" he answered, which made my brother Roberto want to give him a good whack, and he didn't do it only because he was holding a croissant in each hand.

Then the Captain of the Firemen, furious at such insolence, summoned up all his authority and said:

"You either help, you naughty pup, or mark my words, we'll lock you up."

"That's right, that's right," said the Ambassadors in unison.

The boy was alarmed and replied:

"Fine, what do you want me to do?"

"First," said the Superintendent, "tell us whether any of the last few kites flown have got tangled up with any elephants or Firemen."

"But are you all totally barking mad?" asked the boy. "When have you ever seen a flying elephant?"

"Never," I replied, "but it turns out Dailan Kifki isn't like other elephants. And we can't just allow him to remain lost in the sky without anyone to make him his lovely oats soup."

Right there, I started to cry on the shoulder of my Auntie Clodomira, who had to open her umbrella.

The Captain went back to being all authoritative again and said:

"We need to fly kites urgently until we have rescued our astronauts from the skies of the Fatherland!"

"Fine, very well," said the Secretary, resigned. And he ran off, whistling through his fingers to gather his fellows from the Union.

We sat down on the grass and waited patiently for him to return.

14

Loads of boys appeared all at once, each filthier and more ragged than the last, pulling behind them dozens of sumptuous-looking kites.

We all applauded and said "Oooooh!" at the beauty of the kites. Everyone, that is, except for Granddad, who objected:

"Well, that's a fine way to behave! Flying kites when you're supposed to be practising your times tables!"

When the whole gang had assembled, the Secretary of the Union made us line up and, marking time, we all marched over to a neighbouring paddock and got ready to fly the famous kites.

Meanwhile word had got around Ituzaingó that a whole lot of important people were fishing for an elephant in the sky, which meant that an enormous number of busybodies began to descend on us to take a look. The schools proclaimed an official holiday, and various schoolteachers and principals appeared with their pupils. The priest also arrived, absolutely furious, having come to fetch his escaped altar boys. Kids on bicycles came too, and milkmen in their carts, gentlemen in cars, a dog with two tails, countryfolk on horseback and several sheep on foot.

Suddenly we heard some lovely music. Naturally, it was the Boy Scouts' band. There was a volley of cannon-fire, and we all started flying kites.

We were so happy that for a moment we forgot that our aim was to find Dailan Kifki and the Fireman, who were shipwrecked in the sky.

The sun was shining brightly, and there was a lovely breeze.

There were peanut sellers, wafer sellers and ice-cream sellers.

In short, there was everything we could have wanted.

Granddad went off to sulk by the wire fence, grumbling to himself, but when nobody was looking he started flying a kite, too.

But he was so unlucky at it that his kite dragged him off and picked him up and carried him into the air.

"*Ker-BLAM!*" I said.

"We're toast," said my brother Roberto.

"Now what if Granddad flies off and we'll have to fish for him, too?" said my dad.

Fortunately Granddad got caught on a eucalyptus tree and the Captain, with his ladder, went up to rescue him.

The moment Granddad came back down to earth, he started lecturing us on *How to Fly a Kite*.

Anyway, we worked all morning, and we were just about ready to give up because there was no trace of Dailan Kifki anywhere in the sky, when the Captain decided to climb a tree and look out from there with a telescope, to see whether he could spot them flying behind a cloud, or sitting, roasting hot, on the sun. We were already giving up all hope of recovering our astronauts when the Captain shouted:

"Haaaaaaalt! There they go! Fly those kites on the double! One—two!"

We were off in a flash. In our haste all our lines got tangled up and some of us knocked into one another with a real bump.

And that was when I saw them!

There, all the way up there, far away amid the clouds... There they flew: Dailan Kifki and the Fireman.

15

We started such an uproar when we spotted Dailan Kifki that the Manager of the Ituzaingó Post Office came running over, furious, because all his stamps had come unstuck.

The crowd of busybodies was growing. Some were yelling, others were placing bets.

"I'll bet you three chocolates they won't catch them," one was saying.

"I'll bet you three caramels that they will!" said another.

"Higher, Dailan Kifki, don't let them catch you!" shouted one.

"Work those kites, don't let them get away!" shouted another.

And however much Granddad may have wanted to maintain discipline, holding up a baton in an attempt to keep order, he could not shut them up.

I was afraid the noise would scare Dailan Kifki.

We already had aching arms and quite bad cricks in our necks from so much kite-flying, but the elephant went on fluttering about like a fat butterfly, fooling around, turning somersaults, always just a little higher than the kites, so all our efforts were in vain.

"Dailan Kifki!" I shouted up to him, "why don't you fly a little lower, sweetie?"

No response from him at all.

The Mini-Secretary of Aeronautics started shouting instructions to the Fireman.

"Mister Fireman, come down, switch off the engines, turn to the right, bank towards the west. It's time you had a rest. Truly, it's for the best!"

No response from the Fireman either.

Some big lads climbed a eucalyptus tree and started throwing stones at him. A lot of us had to give up our kites for a bit to go get those meanies under control. Granddad climbed the tree and started chasing them along the branches. They looked like a tribe of monkeys.

But the worst of it was that the Ambassadors started squabbling. And my mum could find nothing better to do than sidle over to me and tell me in my ear:

"Listen, my girl, I do hope that when the Fireman gets down you are going to marry him, aren't you?"

"But Mum," I replied indignantly, "do you really think I'm only trying to fish him down so I can marry him?"

"Why not? He's a fine fellow, and very brave," my mum insisted.

"That's enough, Mum," I said. "I don't want to get married, I just want to get Dailan Kifki back."

"But you can't be thinking of marrying an elephant!" replied Mum. "That I simply will not allow. What would the neighbours say? What would Auntie Clodomira say? And above all, what would Granddad say, because I'm quite sure the elephant can't read or write."

"That's enough, Mum," I said, impatiently. "Stop that now, I'm busy."

Then my mother wandered off whimpering and complaining at the top of her lungs so that everyone could hear her:

"Ay ay ay, such terrible misfortune! My daughter wants to marry an elephant!"

You cannot imagine the stir this caused among the audience.

They immediately started placing bets: *She will marry him, she won't marry him, she will she won't she won't she will...*

And my mum, who hadn't understood a thing, went off to fetch Granddad to try and persuade me against it.

"Wherever have you heard of such an idea?" Granddad was telling me off. "When have you ever seen a young lady marrying an ignorant elephant, huh?"

"But Granddad," I said, "why on earth would you believe I'd want to marry an elephant? Mum just misunderstood. That wasn't what I said."

"If that's what she said, there had to be a reason," replied my granddad, and then added, "I'm telling you right now I don't approve of this marriage. You must marry a qualified schoolteacher or, even better, a university professor."

"Yes, very well, Granddad. But please, leave me alone now. My kite is getting tangled and Dailan Kifki is going to get away."

Of course, in the meantime the rumour had spread and the journalists arrived, and the TV newsreader and the photographers. They approached me with their cameras and bits of paper and pencils in their hands, asking questions:

"Is it true, miss, that you're fishing for an elephant in order to marry him?"

"Of course not," I said desperately, "the very idea is utterly preposterous!"

And since they couldn't hear very well with all that commotion, they wrote down "rhinoceros" instead of "preposterous".

"It's a bombshell!" another shouted. "For the first time in history, a young woman is going to marry an elephant!"

"Is the groom going to wear a top hat for the wedding?" one of them asked.

"Will you be spending your honeymoon at the zoo?"

Then, fortunately, my Auntie Clodomira scared them off with blows from her umbrella, saying:

"No sir, absolutely not, we don't approve of this marriage, not in the least."

I moved away, utterly fed up with the whole mess, and went on flying my kite.

Dailan Kifki was still floating in the sky, without any sign that he might be getting tired. But when I looked closely I could see his wings were in a wretched state: all the buttons and bows had come untied, the silver-paper trimmings were worn ragged, the tulle was quite moth-eaten, and the rosette had come off. I didn't think he'd be able to go on flying very much longer in that condition.

My brother Roberto just kept shaking his head as he watched him, saying over and over:

"We're toast."

My Auntie Clodomira threatened him with her umbrella.

My father signalled towards him with his pipe, as though indicating which way to land.

And at that moment a huge collective disaster happened.

16

Oh yes, a huge disaster.

Several people, including Granddad and the Ambassadors, wanted to sit down for a bit on the grass to rest and... they had to sit down with their arms up in the air! They had all become stiff from flying their kites for so long and they couldn't bring them down!

I tried to move Granddad's arm back into place, but it was as though it had turned to stone.

"It's an outrage!" Granddad said. "It's like I'm permanently asking permission to come up to the front of the class."

Fortunately at that very moment we heard a siren, horn blasts and a noisy squeal of brakes.

It was the ambulance.

Out came five lovely doctors and three lovely dentists, all in starched white, with carnations in their ears. They were carrying little saws, screwdrivers, bottles, scissors, bandages, hammers and erasers.

They immediately began to see to the patients and, using cough syrup and a screwdriver, managed to get their arms back down.

Naturally, the doctors and dentists then started flying kites themselves, too.

We kept on trying to fish the astronauts down, until my brother Roberto had a brilliant idea.

He called me to one side with a mysterious look on his face and whispered:

"I bet Dailan Kifki's getting hungry."

"Of course he is, he's starving!" I answered, "But I'm sure he doesn't want to come down, for fear we'll tell him off."

"I know what will make him land," said my brother Roberto, still sounding mysterious.

"So what should we be doing?" I asked, intrigued.

"Making lovely oats soup," he replied. "As soon as he smells it, he'll be zooming back down to earth before you know it."

"And how are we going to make lovely oats soup here in the middle of the countryside?" I asked.

"Let's ask Granddad," he replied. "He used to be a Boy Scout. He knows how to solve these problems."

And off we went to ask Granddad how we might be able to make lovely oats soup in the middle of the countryside.

"The kind of oats soup made with water or with milk?" asked Granddad.

"With milk, of course!" we replied.

"Then it's very simple," replied Granddad. "You put six kilos of oats in a saucepan—"

"But we haven't got any oats," I said.

"Or a saucepan," added Roberto.

"Then you'll have to plant some oats," said Granddad, "and while they're growing, you can ask if one of the Ambassadors will lend you his top hat and we'll use that as a saucepan."

Granddad really is very clever.

He immediately set about planting oats while my brother and I, on tiptoes and ever so quiet, went to try and get the top hat off the head of one of the Ambassadors without his noticing.

Luckily one of them was half asleep, leaning up against the trunk of a tree, so we approached him from behind and started to take off his top hat.

It wasn't easy, because the top hat was too small for him and he was wearing it wedged down quite tightly. But at last we managed it.

"Hooray, we've got our saucepan!" yelled my brother Roberto.

"Just a moment," I said. "When Mister Ambassador wakes up and feels the sun on the top of his bald head he'll get angry, and he's going to realise we've stolen his top hat."

So the two of us hurriedly wove a top hat out of eucalyptus leaves and pulled it down onto his head, nice and slow so as not to wake him.

A beautiful, scented top hat—and good for a cough, too!

Granddad was looking pleased at how well the oats were growing.

"We've got our saucepan," we said.

As grumpy as ever, he glanced at it out the corner of his eye and muttered:

"Well, it's not great, but in the country you have to make do with whatever you've got."

He immediately sent my brother Roberto off to light the fire.

"I haven't got any matches," said Roberto. "How should I do it?"

"Like the natives, ignorant child!" answered my granddad, shooting him a thunderous look.

And so we started rubbing two stones together to make sparks, while Granddad gathered twigs and dry leaves.

It was pretty hard work, but finally—like two hours later—we managed to light a decent fire.

Naturally, as soon as we'd lit it, Granddad discovered he had a box of matches in his pocket for lighting his pipe.

In the meantime the oats had grown, so we threw them into the saucepan—that is, into the Ambassador's top hat.

I looked up at the sky. Nothing had changed: Dailan Kifki was fluttering about looking perfectly calm, the Fireman was still on Dailan Kifki's head, and everyone was trying to fish them down with their kites.

Our only remaining hope was that the yummy smell of lovely oats soup might tempt him and they'd fly a little lower to smell it better.

But then...

17

We were just about to put the oat-filled top hat over the fire (some distance away, so it wouldn't singe) when we realised we were still missing the main ingredient: milk.

And there wasn't a milkman anywhere to be seen in the crowd.

"How are we going to make lovely oats soup without any milk?" I asked, desperate.

"I think I saw a cow out there somewhere," said Granddad.

"Yes, I saw one too," added my brother Roberto.

"Where, where?" we all asked, scanning the horizon, shading our eyes with our hands.

Finally *waaaaaaay* off in the distance I thought I could see some horns.

"There's one!" I shouted.

"Get her!" ordered Granddad, grabbing hold of his butterfly net.

"Milk her!" bellowed my brother Roberto, who hadn't the slightest idea of how one milks a cow.

And off the three of us ran.

After, like, a mile of running, the three of us had to turn right around again because we realised we hadn't brought the container for the milk.

We came back for the top hat, then raced off again, fast as the devil.

W e approached the cow slowly, really slowly, the three of us hand in hand, absolutely terrified.

I elbowed Granddad and said:

"You talk to her, Granddad, you're the biggest. She won't pay any attention to me."

Granddad elbowed my brother Roberto and said:

"You talk to her, you're the youngest."

And my brother elbowed me and said:

"You talk to her, you're a woman."

So there we were, the three of us, hand in hand, looking at the cow, the cow looking at us (with great curiosity), and no one getting up the nerve to ask permission to milk her, so that we'd have a little bit of milk for preparing Dailan Kifki's soup.

No one!

Finally I summoned up my courage, cleared my throat, straightened out my dress and, showing I was the bravest of the three, I said to the cow:

"Good afternoon, Mrs Cow."

The cow looked at me, very alert, and replied:

"*Moo.*"

I tried to make a bit of small talk to distract her, because of course you can't simply come along expecting to milk a cow just like that.

And so I said:

"What a lovely day, isn't it, Mrs Cow?"

And she—very alert—nodded and said again insistently:

"*Moo.*"

Granddad elbowed me and muttered:

"Get on with it then, we've got to start the milking."

So I scratched the cow's ear, just a bit, and asked sweetly:

"I wonder whether you might permit us, oh noble Mrs Cow, to take a nice little bit of milk from you?"

The cow, still very alert, nodded and said again:

"*Moo.*"

"I'll handle this," said Granddad.

And he started to milk her, while my brother Roberto held the top hat and I went on stroking behind her ear, so she wouldn't get scared.

Once we had filled the top hat, we thanked her, bowing low, and the cow replied with a wave of her little tail.

When we put the soup back on the fire, Granddad kept himself busy telling half the world that all on his own he'd tamed a ferocious wild cow in the forests of Ituzaingó.

What do you say to that!

18

I was stirring the soup with a branch.

My brother Roberto, from time to time, would put a finger into the top hat and taste it.

The delicious scent of lovely oats soup with milk was starting to rise up towards the sky, with just a hint of toasted top hat...

The smell was so delicious that a whole load of busybodies came over, my Auntie Clodomira among others. Everyone wanted to try it.

Everyone was sniffing at it so hard, inhaling so deeply, that we had to get rid of them.

"On you go, on you go, get out of here, at this rate you won't leave the tiniest drop of soup smell left for Dailan Kifki," we said.

Since they didn't go, I had to ask the Superintendent for help, and using his whistle, his truncheon and his white gloves he managed to move the busybodies away and get them to stand over by the wire fence.

Every once in a while, still stirring the soup, I glanced up at the sky.

Dailan Kifki and the Fireman were still fluttering about, but soon the aroma of soup got stronger and I noticed Dailan Kifki looking down and stretching out his trunk to smell it better.

"Prepare the kites!" commanded Granddad.

Everyone started flying their kites, and gathered them close to one another right by the voyagers.

My brother Roberto was blowing on the fire and his face was getting covered in soot and smoke.

I stirred more and more excitedly and blew the steam up towards the sky.

It really was a great idea: Dailan Kifki just could not resist.

He started to fly in circles around the paddock, at a very low altitude.

Finally some people were able to tangle him in their kites.

You wouldn't believe how much we cheered and applauded.

Nice and slowly, they began to lower the kites, and with them Dailan Kifki and the Fireman, who still had their eyes fixed on the soup.

They came gliding down, down, down...

Finally Dailan Kifki came to a gentle landing, sweetly, like marmalade, like a little feather, like a piece of fluff, like a dandelion abandoned by the breeze on a sandy beach...

And yes—it just so happened that Dailan Kifki came down to earth right beside the lovely oats soup.

The crowd fell into an incredible silence...

Then, majestically, Dailan Kifki approached the top hat, plunged in his trunk and drank up all the soup without stopping to take a breath.

I was so overwhelmed that I had to stifle a little cough in my collar.

19

But don't think for a moment that our troubles were over once Dailan Kifki had landed.

Nope.

They were only just beginning.

You have no idea how complicated it is to keep an elephant!

I'd advise you never to try keeping such a big creature—to be satisfied with a pussycat, instead, or a doggywog, or a tweetybird. It's simpler, and cheaper, and after all, any one of those can be a most affectionate pet.

Well, as I was saying, Dailan Kifki landed, and drank up all his soup in one gulp, while the Fireman remained up on top, posing for the photographers and the news cameras.

The Fireman was so dizzy with his success that he hadn't noticed what was happening to the soup.

But when he saw that Dailan Kifki had drunk it all for himself, what do you think he did? He started to cry!

I didn't know what was wrong with him, so I asked the Captain of the Firemen, who answered:

"He's feeling very sad-sad-sad that all the soup's been had-had-had."

"Oh, the shame!" I said. "Such a big, strong Fireman crying over a bit of an elephant's lovely oats soup. Mister Captain, tell him to dismount and help us with all the many things we've got to do, instead of crying like a baby."

So the Captain squared up in front of the Fireman, saluted and gave the order:

"Mister Fireman, don't delay, get off that creature *right away!*"

But do you know what that ill-mannered Fireman replied?

"I won't get off here if you yell. 'Cos I want *my* oats soup as well."

"Can't you see there's none left?" I said.

Then my mother came over and said:

"Really, my girl, when you marry this Fireman, I think you're going to have to make him lovely oats soup every blessed day."

"I have no intention of marrying a cry-baby Fireman!" I replied.

The Fireman didn't want to get down off Dailan Kifki's head, so to prevent another escape I started removing the elephant's wings.

I untied the ribbons, unstuck the bits of paper, and cut the pieces of twine, because if he kept the wings on I was sure they'd fly away again.

If only I hadn't done that.

When Dailan Kifki realised I was taking off his wings he began to cry like twenty elephants who had peeled twenty tons of onions.

Naturally, before long the Manager of the Ituzaingó Post Office showed up, furiouser than ever, because the commotion had unstuck all the stamps again.

This business with the stamps was beginning to get on my nerves.

20

I'd always thought that when Dailan Kifki and the Fireman landed safe and sound we'd have a party and there would be great happiness, a national holiday, a cannon-volley salute, a musical band and fireworks.

There wasn't.

There was just a lot of terrible weeping. Everyone cried so much that the paddock began to flood and my Auntie Clodomira ran this way and that with her open umbrella.

The Fireman was crying because there wasn't even a drop of soup left for him.

Dailan Kifki was crying because I'd taken off his wings and he wouldn't be doing any more flying.

The Captain of the Firemen was crying because the Fireman wouldn't get down off the elephant.

Granddad was crying because nobody would let him make a speech.

My mum was crying because I didn't want to marry the Fireman.

But there was one person who was crying harder than anyone else: the Ambassador whose top hat we'd stolen!

We had been intending to give it a good clean and return it once the soup was done.

But we didn't.

We couldn't.

Because as it turned out, Dailan Kifki had been so hungry that after drinking all the soup he'd eaten the top hat too, biting through it *cranch crinch crunch* as though it were a wafer or an ice cream cone.

By the time I noticed, all that was left of the top hat was the ribbon.

The Ambassador wasn't satisfied with that, of course, and even threatened to declare war and everything.

I tried to keep perfectly calm, but I kept seeing so many other people crying that my own bottom lip was starting to quiver.

By now it was already late, we'd completed our rescue mission and it was time to think about heading home.

More and more busybodies kept arriving, and more photographers.

There wasn't one person, even with so many authorities around, who could keep everyone in order.

Until my Auntie Clodomira gave the command to the Superintendent. And the Superintendent then straightened his cap, did his jacket up smartly, gave his buttons a good shine with his sleeve, put on his white gloves, which were pretty well black by this point, grabbed hold of his truncheon, blew on his whistle and with his arms spread wide ordered everybody to *STOP CRYING*.

At once a great silence reigned, such a great silence that the paddock felt like a church.

The altar boys brought their hands together and rolled their eyes heavenward.

And in the middle of this amazing silence, we could hear— from far, far away—a very tuneful little melody.

Everyone looked out towards the horizon.

We saw a huge cloud of dust and heard the galloping of many horses.

The music grew.

All of a sudden, our jaws dropped.

21

We couldn't close our mouths.

You won't believe me, but it's true.

A lovely carriage drawn by ten white horses!

"Could it be the Queen of England?" I wondered. "But how could she have heard about the adventure of Dailan Kifki so fast and come all the way to Ituzaingó by carriage?"

"Who could it be?" everyone started to ask.

Granddad prepared for war.

"Atten...*shun!*" he shouted. "Everyone put on your overalls!"

Everyone did as they were told. Of course, none of them actually had any overalls because they weren't at school, but everyone smoothed down their clothes, combed their fingers through their hair, shook off a few bits of fluff, did up their buttons, straightened their top hats and lined up in rows with the most serious expressions they had, to receive the dazzling and mysterious visitors.

Someone suggested that since we'd spent so many days coming and going and so many nights without so much as forty winks, maybe we were just seeing things, like those travellers in the desert.

But it turns out we weren't.

The carriage was getting closer and closer. And it was real.

It was a real carriage made entirely of gold, and little pearls, except for the mudguards, which were plastic.

The horses were real, too: all of them made of one hundred per cent horse, twirling their very long curly manes, dyed green, pink and yellow.

The carriage braked right in front of Dailan Kifki, and my brother Roberto said:

"We're toast."

The soldiers stood to attention and saluted, just in case.

Granddad presented arms.

My Auntie Clodomira was convinced that it was the President of the Republic inside that carriage, but that sounded a bit strange to me, as I know the President doesn't travel by carriage, nor by skateboard, but by car or helicopter.

The carriage just stood there, with its doors and windows closed.

And the horses were calm and still, as though their clockwork had suddenly wound down.

22

Finally my Auntie Clodomira couldn't take it any longer and raced purposefully over to the carriage to see who our famous visitors were.

The moment she opened the door, out leapt a little dwarf.

Yes, a dwarf just like a real one in a story: with a coloured hat, a white beard, and looking terrifically grouchy. But there was one other thing. He looked different from other famous dwarves because he was dressed like a footballer.

His beard came down over his T-shirt, so I couldn't tell what his team was. I could only make out the little shorts and the big boots.

My Auntie Clodomira gave a disappointed sigh.

"Pah," she said, "such a big carriage for such a small dwarf."

"Shhh," I said, "he might hear you and get annoyed."

The grouchy dwarf stamped his little feet two or three times, then—without looking at anyone or saying hello politely, which annoyed Granddad—he marched straight over to Dailan Kifki.

He barely came up to the elephant's knees, and started jumping up in the air to pull on his ears, but he couldn't reach.

So I picked him up and the little dwarf stroked Dailan Kifki's ears very happily.

Then he showed his gratitude by smiling at me.

I said: "Welcome, Mister Dwarf."

And he replied: "*Supisichi.*" Which in dwarf language means something or other. I honestly have no idea what.

"I want to ride around on the elephant," he added straight away, whimsically and now in perfect Spanish.

No one dared contradict him, seeing as he was such an important little dwarf who travelled around in a carriage and who was probably a little football champion. And so between us we all lifted him up and placed him on Dailan Kifki's head.

He rode around a few times, smiling and greeting people and making great flourishes with his hat.

"Right then, that's it, I've had my ride around now," he said three hours later. But he hadn't ridden around us just once. He'd done it fifteen thousand times, and Dailan Kifki was extremely dizzy.

We were all dying of curiosity, whispering to each other about who the mysterious dwarf might be. We were afraid he might run off again in his carriage without telling us about himself, or even his name.

That was what we were all thinking, when suddenly he looked at each of us in turn—it took quite some time—and finally asked us, crossly:

"And you people, who are you?"

At first nobody dared answer, as though we had all forgotten who we were.

So I introduced them.

The dwarf, listening very carefully, took off his hat and shook hands with each of us in turn. There were so many of us that just this saying hello took him something like five hours and fourteen minutes.

After this introduction I felt I had the right to ask him myself who he was. I cleared my throat, smoothed down my pinafore and straightened my tulle hat with the little flags, which was in a wretched state. Making a low bow I asked him:

"And now might we perhaps know who you are, Mister Dwarf, sir?"

"What do you mean, who I am?" he answered, furious. "Is it possible you don't know who I am?"

"No, I'm ever so sorry, Mister Dwarf, sir. I've never seen you before."

"Such ignorance!" he remarked, hopping about with annoyance.

I decided to ask Granddad, who is so wise.

"Granddad, do you know who he is?"

Granddad answered:

"He can't be anybody, because I've never seen him in any history books, or geography books, or botany books, or books of phantasmagorical astronautics... not even drawn in a comic strip."

And because the dwarf was so silent and pensive, looking down at his boots and not telling us who he was, we all became fascinated. And we too just kept looking down and squeezing little eucalyptus leaves with nervous fingers.

23

"Very well," said the dwarf half an hour later, "if someone could pick me up, I shall tell you who I am."

The Captain hurried to pick him up delicately, and when he was up, feeling much taller now, the dwarf coughed a little, straightened his hat and said solemnly:

"I am the dwarf Carozo Minujín, Owner and Lord of the Forest of Gulubú."

"Aaaahh..." we all said with a round of applause, even though we'd never heard of the Forest of Gulubú.

At that moment Granddad took a step forward, grabbed the dwarf by the nose, and said:

"You're a liar!"

"A liar? Me?" roared the dwarf, furious.

"Yes, you," insisted Granddad. "I've spent my whole life studying geography and I've never seen any forest or country or lake or corner or football pitch called Gulubú. It's all lies!"

The dwarf started flapping his hands about to try and hit Granddad, but he couldn't reach him.

"This Gulubú forest of yours does not exist!" screamed Granddad. "Show me, go on! Point it out on the map of the Argentine Republic. Well? Let's see it, then."

"Me, point it out to you? No *supisichi* way!" roared the

dwarf. "The Forest of Gulubú doesn't appear on any maps, sir, and that's all there is to it."

"Ah," replied Granddad, "so you'd have me believe that a forest that doesn't appear on any maps really is a forest?"

"Yes, sir. And if you like I'll take you there and show it to you."

I thought: How delightful, the little dwarf is going to take us in his carriage to see a forest that doesn't exist on any maps!

But my grouchy old granddad seemed determined to rain on our parade, because he just kept stamping his feet and saying over and over:

"No sir, I'm not going to some inferior little forest that isn't on any maps."

"Inferior?" screamed the dwarf. "Did you say inferior? Well, how can it be in Ferior, sir, if it's right here in Argentina? Well, what do you say to that?"

Which was a good point.

"Well, if it's not an inferior little forest, it must be a rubbish little forest," grumbled Granddad, who was not prepared to give in.

And then... Oh, I'd rather not remember what happened next!

The little dwarf Carozo Minujín drew a sword! Naturally it wasn't a very big sword, but it did look really sharp. Right then and there he challenged Granddad to a duel for having insulted his lovely forest.

"Come on now, don't quarrel," I said. But the dwarf flapped his arms about until he had got free of the Captain, and landed firmly on the ground.

"Let me at him," said Granddad. "Let me at him to defend my honour—and more importantly, the honour of geography!"

And right there they started to fight. *Chiss, chass, clink, clank!* went their swords. The little dwarf, his face flushed with rage, muttered again and again through gritted teeth:

"*Supisichi supisichi supisichi.*"

It was like a musketeer movie. They leapt about, twirled, skipped and somersaulted.

Until Granddad got tired, because to be frank he is an old man, and asked for a temporary truce. He went off to rest a bit beneath a eucalyptus tree.

The dwarf put his sword away beneath his beard and said:

"I have won a great victory. I deserve to be picked up to greet this audience."

My Auntie Clodomira picked him up and he raised both his arms to greet the crowds, who cheered his name:

"Long live Mister Little Dwarf Carozo Minujín!", which made him blush with pleasure.

Then he said solemnly:

"Now I invite you all to come for some hot chocolate at my palace in the Forest of Gulubú, so you can see it really does exist."

"Let's go, let's go!" cried everyone except Granddad, as we were all desperate to take a carriage ride and drink hot chocolate in an unknown forest.

And do you know what the Fireman (who was still sulking) said?

He just made this ridiculous comment:

"Oats soup is quite the only thing that really makes me smile. I don't like going places, and hot chocolate is vile!"

Would you believe it?

24

Little Mister Carozo Minujín led me by the hand to his carriage. I was about to get in when I heard a huge commotion behind me.

Ker-BLAM!

I said, "Another problem."

The Secretary of the Union of Kite-Flyers was screeching like a demon.

"You owe us for lots and lots of hours of work!" he complained. "We've been flying kites for three days now, to fish for this calamity of an elephant, and now you're just going to go off without paying us!"

"You're quite right, of course," I replied. "The thing is, we all thought you fished for elephants for free."

"Absolutely not," he said, handing me a dirty scrap of paper covered in numbers. It was the bill: *65 pesos, 20 cents.*

"Either you pay us," he grumbled, "or we put the elephant back up."

Everyone began rummaging through their pockets, but Mister Dwarf was too quick for us and drew out a purse made of a caterpillar cocoon from which he took two square gold coins. At the same time he also took out a circular handkerchief to blow his nose.

The Secretary was very pleased with the coins, and didn't bother us any more.

Finally I boarded the carriage and then I really did have quite a surprise. Because the carriage was very big on the outside but rather tiny on the inside, since it was made to measure for its owner. On the inside it was very luxurious, all lined in silver paper and with a few photos of the great comic actor Charlie Chaplin and the great tango singer Charlie Gardel stuck on the ceiling. But it was really very tiny for me. I had to be all crumpled up and squeezed like a walnut, my hat pressed against the roof. I didn't even have enough space for smiling in without a bit of my mouth escaping out the window. I had to put one foot on top of the other and one hand on top of the other and both hands on top of my head because there was nowhere else to put them.

Mister Carozo sat down beside me and asked, hospitably: "Comfy?"

I answered yes with a little smile, so as not to offend him, but hoped with all my heart that the journey wouldn't be too long.

The other people followed us, either on foot or riding on Dailan Kifki. Honestly, the poor thing had well over, like, a thousand seven hundred and eighty people on his head and back.

From time to time Mister Dwarf would invite me to admire the scenery, but I have to admit I couldn't see a thing because the carriage windows were so small on the inside it was like looking through a keyhole.

So I sighed with relief when at last the horses stopped snorting and Mister Dwarf said contentedly:

"This is where it starts: my Forest of Gulubú."

25

Mister Dwarf Carozo Minujín hopped out of the carriage and politely offered his hand to help me down after him.

I unrolled myself as best I could and jumped down onto the ground. I looked around carefully and then asked, a little disappointed:

"So, *this* is your famous Forest of Gulubú?"

"The very same," he replied, very pleased with himself.

"But I don't see a forest anywhere," I said.

And my companions and my family and the busybodies all joined in:

"We don't see a forest anywhere! Why have you brought us all this way?"

"*Supisichi,*" replied the dwarf, which calmed us down a great deal.

When we were *all* just about ready to have our bottom lips start quivering, the little dwarf took a few steps forward and said some magic words, which were:

"*Chipiti-chapiti-bampiti-boom...*"

... or something like that, I think. He walked over to some pieces of wire and pulled. We all thought he was crazy, when we saw him holding on to some quite ordinary wires—just those regular ones that grow wild on a normal wire fence—but we were wrong.

Not only was he not crazy, but the wires were magical, and the moment he pulled them... *Ker-BLAM!*

Have you seen those pop-up books that you open and the characters suddenly stand up inside them?

Well, the Forest of Gulubú is just like that. As if it were filled with sleeping marionettes. You give a little pull on their strings and they're up on their feet, dancing and moving about.

The Forest of Gulubú is ironed flat on the ground, and when its owner pulls on the wires, the trees and the grasses and the cottages and the animals all appear suddenly, as if to say:

"Here we are! We were just playing hide-and-seek."

You can imagine our surprise. My Auntie Clodomira fainted, with pretty good aim this time because she fell right into the arms of the Superintendent.

It's not every day you see a forest rising up from the ground, just like that, in a place where a moment ago there was nothing but a bit of open pasture and which, it would seem, is not all that far from the town of Ituzaingó.

None of us could believe it. We rubbed our eyes and our jaws dropped.

Dailan Kifki was utterly delighted. He knelt down to allow people to dismount from his head and back, using his trunk as a slide. And the moment he felt free of that enormous weight he trotted off into the Forest of Gulubú, no doubt hoping to find himself a banana tree, or a pear tree, or an oats-soup tree.

Meanwhile the rest of us walked into the forest with the dwarf, who wouldn't let go of my hand. He explained that whenever he went off on a trip he would flatten the forest and leave it lying down and invisible so that nobody would steal it or spoil it. I remarked that he was right to do so; it was

worth taking good care of such a handsome forest. Because I must tell you, that Forest of Gulubú isn't just any old forest. It's certainly not some inferior little forest like Granddad said it was.

Not at all. It's very big and very real, like one of those forests that only exist in stories. With trees filled with wise little birds, the kind that aren't just painted but completely alive. With a delightful stream where there are frogs learning to swim, in polka-dot swimming-trunks, and where Dailan Kifki had rushed to give his trunk a drink until Mister Carozo shooed him away, because he was drinking so much he was going to dry it out completely.

In this forest there were toads smoking pipes and big toadstools with fridges and TV sets. Rabbits cycled past, and—strangest of all, I thought—there were canaries with cages. But those birds weren't inside the cages. They were carrying them around like briefcases, filled with all their school equipment.

We were all very happy as we walked through the Forest of Gulubú, breathing in a delicious scent of peppermints, finally having a rest after so much coming and going and turning around and around, when Granddad, as usual, decided to throw cold water on our party.

He stood up on a tree trunk and shouted:

"Quiet, children!"

We all fell silent.

When Granddad saw that the silence was so complete that even the birds were dumbstruck and the canaries had stopped in mid-air to listen to him, he said, solemnly:

"Now that we have arrived in this forest, following a long and arduous voyage through dangerous and unknown regions,

I shall immediately be giving you an illustrated zoology and botany lesson."

I'm sure you can imagine how much we all felt like having a lesson just then, can't you?

My brother Roberto said:

"We're toast."

Once again, I had to admit he was right.

26

W e were getting extremely bored listening to the lesson and waiting patiently for Granddad to finish reciting all these really strange plant and animal names, when suddenly I looked around me and asked in alarm:

"Where's Dailan Kifki?"

I couldn't see him anywhere, and he's definitely too big to go unnoticed or to hide underneath a head of lettuce.

I'd been sitting on the grass like everyone else, yawning *this wide* over Granddad's lesson, and I started to slide away sideways, just very slowly... slowly... so I could escape and go looking for Dailan Kifki before anything serious happened.

Fortunately Granddad was having so much fun busily explaining a snapdragon that he didn't notice me getting away from his lesson. I crawled slowly over to the Fireman, who immediately put himself at my service without even asking what the matter was.

I pulled him away from the crowd till we were out of Granddad's line of sight. We hid behind a cabbage and I asked him in a whisper:

"Where's Dailan Kifki?"

"I on't-day oh-nay..." the Fireman whispered back.

"I'm absolutely sure the little pest has escaped again. We've got to find him!"

Then the Fireman explained, very seriously:

"To find a lonely elephant who's missing in the wood, you need a lot of patience and your senses must be good."

"Yes, that's true," I said, "but you also have to know the terrain very well, and if you ask me we're going to get ourselves lost in this blessed Forest of Gulubú, so we'd do well to find Mister Dwarf Carozo to lead our expedition."

But the really big problem was that Mister Carozo was sitting in the very front row of Granddad's lesson, and to reach him I'd have to go past a whole crowd of people who were sitting all quiet and serious just like at school.

"So what do we do?" I asked the Fireman.

And the Fireman thought for quite some time, frowning, with his finger to his forehead, then replied:

"To remove a dwarf discreetly from your Granddad's class, just look: You take a fishing rod and neatly tie a fishing line and hook."

I thought this was an excellent idea: we'd fish Mister Carozo out without Granddad noticing, because if we were to wait for the break-time bell, we would be toast. Granddad's lessons never last less than five hours.

Since there were no fishing rods around, the Fireman used his axe that shone as bright as the moon to cut off a strong, flexible branch. Since we didn't have any fishing line we used the laces from his boots. And since we didn't have a hook, we used a safety pin that was attached to my pinafore.

When you're in a forest you just have to figure out a way, don't you?

Between us we held the branch tight, and aimed very carefully with a very steady hand, to be absolutely, completely sure we were fishing out the dwarf and not some other person. (Just imagine if we'd fished out my Auntie Clodomira!) And then... *Zzzzzzooooom!* without anybody noticing, Mister Dwarf Carozo was flying towards us through the air on the pin that was tied to the shoelaces which were tied to the branch, and landed safe and sound right beside us.

A terrible shouting broke out behind the cabbage. Mister Dwarf was furious and said some really awful words like "By *sampiolín!*", "*Patatip!*" and "Oh, *tambapatán!*".

The Fireman gagged him with his handkerchief, so that Granddad wouldn't realise we'd fished out one of his students without permission, and like that, all muffled up, he picked him up and between us we carried him farther away, this time behind a pumpkin.

Mister Carozo was still protesting, kicking his feet and waving his arms.

"Do excuse us, Mister Dwarf," I said. "I'm ever so sorry we took you out of the lesson, where I can see you were having such an interesting time..."

"Interesting my foot!" said the dwarf. "I was more bored than a fly!"

"So why are you grumbling so much?" I asked.

"I'm not grumbling because you fished me out," he explained. "I'm grumbling because I was having such a beautiful trip through the air on that fishing line and you brought me down much too soon!"

"Well, if that's the problem," I said kindly, "we can fish you up again so you can keep having fun."

No sooner said than done. We hooked the safety pin onto his T-shirt, and the pin was tied to the shoelace that was tied to the branch, and we twirled him through the air back and forth and back and forth for quite some time.

And Mister Carozo swung from side to side utterly delighted, laughing himself silly because the air was tickling him.

Until the Fireman's arms got tired and he put him back down on the pumpkin.

"More, more!" cried Mister Carozo. But I knelt down and said to him very seriously:

"No, sir. Later we can swing you around as much as you like, but for now you must understand that we only fished you out of class and brought you here so you can help us with a serious, dangerous expedition, and not for these high jinks."

"What's happened?" he asked, in great alarm.

"What's happened is that we've lost Dailan Kifki, and as you are the only person who knows all the nooks and crannies of this forest, you must be our guide to find him."

"And what do you want to find him for?" he asked, combing his beard with his little finger. "He can stay here and live in the forest."

"No, sir," I said emphatically. "Dailan Kifki is mine, and I have to take him back home. And imagine, if he stayed here and one day you decided to flatten down the forest, Dailan Kifki would surely be squashed to death by a tree."

And do you know what the dwarf replied?

"When Granddad's lesson is over, we'll all go to my house for some hot chocolate in pretty little porcelain cups. Then we'll see."

"But it's already getting late," I said, my bottom lip starting to quiver, "and any manner of disaster could happen to Dailan Kifki..."

"*Supisichi*," he said, finally.

And the three of us made our way into the wood, hand in hand in hand: the Fireman, Mister Carozo, and me.

27

We were walking in silence when suddenly Mister Dwarf stopped dead and struck the ground with his heel, like this:

Toc,

　　toc,

　　　　toc.

What could be happening? I wondered.

We soon heard a teeny little high-pitched voice from down on the ground, saying:

"Good evening, my dearest Mister Dwarf Carozo."

I couldn't tell where the voice was coming from. It seemed to be somewhere near my shoes, but since it was already beginning to get dark I couldn't quite make out what was happening down there.

"Good evening to you, Mrs Titina," replied the dwarf.

By crouching all the way down, I could see that the voice was coming from an ant standing at the entrance to her anthill, just about to sweep the threshold with a very—and I mean *very*—small broom.

Titina the Ant, very serious-looking and nicely dressed, with spectacles and an apron.

"What can I do for you?" asked the ant.

"*Supisichi,*" explained Mister Carozo.

"Eep," replied Titina.

"Would you tell us, Mrs Ant, whether by any chance you happened to have seen an elephant passing this way?"

"An ele-*what?*" asked Titina.

"An ele-phant," I explained, impatiently.

"What's one of those?" asked the ant, most curious.

So I tried to explain:

"An elephant is a huge great animal, with four big feet and a trunk and two tusks and a little tail..."

"Does it wear a hat?" Titina interrupted me.

"No, just two very large ears, that's all," I explained.

"In that case, no, I haven't seen one," replied Titina curtly.

"Well, sorry for the trouble, then—thank you anyway," said Mister Carozo. And after giving her a low bow he set off again. We followed him, always hand in hand, feeling Titina's curious look still on our heels.

It was almost dark and we were a bit frightened. We walked on for a while longer when all of a sudden... *Ker-BLAM!* Mister Carozo stopped dead. And fortunately the Fireman and I managed to keep our balance, because if we hadn't, we'd have fallen head-first into a small pond.

Mister Dwarf gave some kind of signal by splashing lightly in the water with the toe of his galoshes, like this:

Plaf,
   plaf,
      plif.

We soon heard a voice answering:

"Ha-ha."

"Good evening, Mrs Frog," said the little man.

And the Frog answered:

"Ha-ha!"

"We're sorry to trouble you, but we just wanted to ask whether by any chance you happened to see an elephant going by?"

And the Frog answered:

"Ha-ha."

Convinced that the poor Frog must have gone crazy from so much splashing around in the pond, we didn't ask her any more, and after waving her goodbye with our shoes, we walked on.

"There's one other person who could give us information," said Mister Carozo.

"Isn't everybody already asleep by this time of night, or nearly?" I asked.

"Oh, no," he replied, "this is someone who's awake all night, singing away, and that is the someone we're going to ask about Dailan Kifki." Then he added "*Supisichi*," which reassured me a great deal.

Finally we arrived at the home of this character, who was the famous Mister Cricket Supreme. He was singing a *zamba* he'd just composed, which went under the title *Cric cric crickiti cric crickiticri cric-cric*.

We couldn't interrupt him right in the best bit of the concert, so we had to wait quite some time, as the *zamba* was a long one.

When he finished he took a bow, and the three of us clapped very loudly, which delighted Mister Cricket, as you can imagine. Because—and I don't know why this is—normally nobody ever claps crickets when they finish singing. Or is it because they never normally finish?

Anyway, just when Mister Dwarf opened his mouth to ask after Dailan Kifki, Mister Cricket started up singing again, this time a *chacarera* he'd just composed, which went under the title *Crickiticric cric cric so-very-much-cric cric*. He wanted us to tell him whether we liked it.

We had to listen carefully to the *chacarera*, which lasted, like, an hour and a half.

Several times I had to nudge the Fireman with my elbow to wake him, because he'd fallen asleep on my shoulder, and his snoring was drowning out the voice of Mister Cricket Supreme. I stayed awake, even though the song did make me feel pretty sleepy. But I didn't sleep, because I was worried about Dailan Kifki. Time was passing and we still hadn't found him.

Finally Mister Cricket ended his *chacarera*, bowed, and then without a moment's hesitation Mister Carozo quickly asked him whether he happened to have seen an elephant going by.

"Of course I saw him," replied Mister Cricket Supreme. "And what's more, I had an argument with him. I gave him such a number of punches on the nose! Honestly, I gave him a serious beating." Which honestly left me with a serious impression that Mister Cricket was a bit of a fibber.

"Why did you have an argument?" I asked, very curious.

"Because he nearly trod on me!" replied Mister Cricket Supreme. "But I gave him, like, a thousand punches on the nose!"

"And who won?" I asked, curious to hear how far his lies might go.

"Me, of course!" replied Mister Cricket.

"Congratulations," I said, not wanting to contradict him. "I don't suppose you might know where that elephant is now?"

"He must be in hospital," replied the liar. "In any case, you should ask Butterfly Lolita, because he went off with her."

"Very well. Goodnight then, Mister Supreme, and thank you for the concert," we said. And we set off again to look for this Butterfly Lolita who, it would seem, had befriended Dailan Kifki.

We stumbled along, nearly dead from exhaustion, till we reached a place which, according to Mister Carozo, was where the butterflies lived. All we could make out was a bit of blue air between the trees, but he insisted it really was the home of the butterflies. Mister Carozo started clicking his fingers and calling them one at a time, by name, but the butterflies didn't appear.

"Where can they have got to?" Mister Carozo wondered. "There are, like, three thousand four hundred and fifty-three of them, and not one has stayed behind to look after the house!"

And then all of a sudden we heard, just a bit farther away, a whispering which sounded like the wind tuning up through the trees. But when we listened more closely, we could clearly make out little butterfly laughs, butterfly smiles and butterfly giggles. Yes, the sound was coming from the butterflies themselves. Neither cats nor giraffes nor cicadas make a sound like that when they laugh.

The three of us, hand in hand, ran towards the place the voices were coming from and there, on the very edge of the Forest of Gulubú, lit up specially by a star which had come unhooked from the sky, what do you think we saw?

Just guess...

28

The butterflies were playing. They were jumping about and tickling each other, running through the air and playing tag. And it wasn't only the star lighting them up, because nine hundred and sixty-five fireflies had also been invited to the party.

And do you know where they were playing, all these butterflies and all these fireflies?

On a tree trunk?

No.

On a toadstool?

No.

On the bank of a stream?

Well, OK, yes. But no.

They were playing and jumping around on Dailan Kifki's back, and he was laughing with sheer delight!

What do you think of that!

I gave him a good telling-off, as was entirely appropriate, and Mister Carozo gave him a smack just below his knee, because he couldn't reach any higher.

"Aren't you ashamed, Dailan Kifki, to be playing around like this while we've been running around desperately looking for you all over the forest?"

"And what's more, *supisichi!*" Mister Carozo added emphatically.

"We have to go back to Ituzaingó station right away," I said firmly, "to take the train back to Buenos Aires."

But Dailan Kifki didn't move and the butterflies just went on playing as if nothing were happening at all.

"Come on," I said again, "you've had your fun."

No response.

"Come now, get a move on, don't delay! Elephant, we haven't got all day," said the Fireman.

Nothing! It was as if Dailan Kifki were glued to the ground.

I pushed him. All three of us pushed him.

Nothing.

Mister Carozo started tugging on his trunk.

Nothing.

"What can we do?" I asked, exhausted. "We can't stay here all night waiting for this elephant to finish playing. Do something, please, Mister Fireman."

So the Fireman spun his polka-dot hose and gave Dailan Kifki a good whack on his rump.

Fortunately, since the hose is made of rubber and so are the polka-dots, it can't have hurt Dailan Kifki too much, but he did feel the slap and took a few steps.

As for the rest of us, we were worried that he might escape again into the forest, so we all three grabbed Dailan Kifki's little tail.

If only we hadn't done that.

In the half-darkness—because the fireflies had turned themselves off just to annoy us—we hadn't noticed that Dailan Kifki was walking into a big puddle.

And in the three of us fell: Mister Dwarf Carozo, the Fireman, and me. Down we went, the three of us, into the mud.

You can't imagine how the butterflies laughed *hee hee hee* and the fireflies laughed *ho ho ho.*

There we were, the three of us sitting in the mud. But let me tell you, we still hadn't let go of Dailan Kifki's tail, so he couldn't possibly get away.

We were pulling so hard on his tail that eventually... *Ker-BLAM!* he also fell in the mud and, of course, as he sat down he spattered us good and proper: our faces, our hair, our necks.

Our bottom lips started to quiver.

Dailan Kifki was too big to pick himself up all on his own, so he just went on sitting there in the mud. And the three of us sat there without moving, too. Just because.

Finally the Fireman, doing various cartwheels and a fine bit of slipping about, managed to get to his feet. He smoothed down his jacket, straightened his helmet and untangled his hose.

I also managed to struggle to my feet without losing my balance. But before anything else, I wanted to clean a bit of the mud off my face, as it was so thick I couldn't so much as wink.

And as I rubbed my hands over my face, my tongue was poking out a little by accident... and...

"What's this?" I said, pleasantly surprised. "This mud tastes quite yummy... Am I dreaming?"

I stuck my tongue out a bit farther and tried it again.

"Oh, quite so. This isn't mud. It's thick chocolate."

And then the fireflies all lit up at once and I saw that Mister Dwarf, who for some reason hadn't spoken in a while, was still sitting in the mud, licking himself nice and clean.

"You're saying this isn't mud, but chocolate?" I asked. "Can that be true?"

"Of course," he replied. "Isn't it a nice idea? In the Forest of Gulubú all the puddles are made of chocolate, or milk and grenadine, or jam, or rice pudding with cinnamon, or raspberry jelly."

"Well, I never knew that, Mister Carozo," I said, before going on to taste another little bit, then another, then another.

Dailan Kifki had finally managed to pick himself up with the help of the Fireman. He had gone back to playing with the butterflies when suddenly he noticed that everyone else was busy tasting the chocolate from the puddle.

If only he hadn't noticed.

First he took just a little with his trunk, and tasted it.

Then he immediately dunked his trunk straight back into the chocolate and didn't take it out again.

"That's enough, Dailan Kifki, you'll get indigestion!" I shouted.

But he went on sucking it up without taking a breath, paying me no notice at all.

Eventually he had sucked up so much so quickly that the puddle was completely dry and, thanks to Dailan Kifki, we were in no danger of drowning, and at no risk of dying of indigestion.

The puddle was all dried out, and the ground beneath it shone like a china plate, having been well slurped, over and over, by Dailan Kifki's trunk.

"*Supisichi,*" said Mister Carozo then. "It's time we went back home for some hot chocolate."

"But how can you even think such a thing?" I asked him indignantly. "How can you imagine we could possibly go on drinking more chocolate?"

"You won't?" replied Mister Carozo, black with rage. "How can you insult me like that? You can't leave the Forest of Gulubú without first stopping by my house to have chocolate in pretty little porcelain cups!"

"Mister Carozo, you've been ever so hospitable, but please try to understand: we've already been away from home for days. We only popped out to fish Dailan Kifki out of the sky, and now that we've done it we can't just wander around the Forest of Gulubú for ever."

"Would you turn down an invitation from the Queen of England?" he asked me with a hard stare.

"No, Mister Carozo," I stammered.

"Would you turn down an invitation from the Shah of Persia?"

"No, Mister Carozo, I wouldn't..."

"Would you turn down an invitation from the Prime Minister of Kenya?"

"Ermmm, no, Mister Carozo..."

"Would you snub Snow White and the Seven Dwarves?"

"Ermmmm, noooo, Mister Carozo."

"Well then, why do you say no to me, and only to me!" he asked, furious, hurling his cap on the ground.

And I understood that we had no choice but to accept his invitation.

In short, a whole other adventure...

So off we went, the three of us, to gather up the rest of the retinue.

We took two or three little steps through the wood, in the darkness, lit only by the fireflies who by now were all half asleep.

We were so tired our feet wouldn't walk for us, our legs wouldn't move us.

So... do you know what Dailan Kifki did?

All on his own, without anyone having to ask him, he knelt down and hoisted us up with his trunk, putting all three of us on top of his head.

And off he trotted, while we hummed the *San Lorenzo March*, but so sleepily it sounded more like the *San Quentin Lullaby*.

29

And that was how we arrived back at the edge of the wood, where Granddad was still teaching his botany lesson. Naturally, everyone else was snoring discreetly.

Granddad was so caught up in his lesson that he didn't even notice us arrive. So we got down off Dailan Kifki and decided we'd also have a quick nap, just till dawn.

I lay down on the grass, with a little pumpkin as my pillow, and was lulled to sleep by the singing of the crickets and the frogs.

I was woken up much later by a bell saying *clang-a-lang-a-lang*.

At first, still half asleep, I thought it was a cowbell. What luck, I thought to myself. Now we'll have milk to make everybody's breakfast, especially Dailan Kifki's lovely oats soup.

But I was wrong.

It wasn't a cow.

It was Granddad ringing the bell for everyone to return to class, in their overalls, with nails clean and faces scrubbed.

Granddad was walking among the sleepers shaking the bell and shouting:

"Right, children, time for class! Break's over! Everyone line up!"

Nobody paid him any attention.

Everyone just turned over and went on grumbling in their sleep, apart from the Fireman who was used to this sort of thing and stood up in his sleep, polished his buttons with his sleeve and gave a salute.

"Well done, student Fireman!" said Granddad, moved at the sight of such an obedient pupil.

I had just woken up, and I was about ready to declare war on Granddad.

When he saw me, he said—without so much as a "Good morning":

"And where is your pencil-case?"

"Granddad," I replied, "we're not at school. This is the Forest of Gulubú, where the puddles are made of chocolate and it's always break-time."

"Everywhere is school!" he answered, furious.

And then he suddenly snapped out of his daze, looked at me and asked:

"Wait...what? What did you say? What are these puddles of chocolate you're talking about?"

"All the pools in the Forest of Gulubú, Granddad."

"They're chocolate?" he said again, squinting with envy. "And those smudges on your face and your pinafore and your ears and your hair—those are from the chocolate?"

"Yes, Granddad."

Then Granddad set about waking everybody up so he could go and give them a chocolate lesson.

Bit by bit, everyone opened one eye, then the other.

My Auntie Clodomira, my brother Roberto, my dad and my mum.

The Captain, the Superintendent, the Ambassadors, the Mini-Secretary, the busybodies, the onlookers, the ice-cream sellers, everyone.

The moment they heard the word "chocolate", they lined up nicely without batting an eyelid.

Granddad was about to lead the new expedition when Mister Carozo interrupted him:

"And where the devil are you going?"

"What do you mean, where am I going?" replied Granddad. "My granddaughter has just told me your forest has lakes filled with chocolate. We are therefore going for a dip."

"No, sir," replied the furious dwarf, "we are absolutely not going for a dip in the pools. We're going to drink hot chocolate at my house, and the way it's supposed to be drunk—out of pretty little porcelain cups on a table."

"I don't want to!" said Granddad, "I'm bored of drinking chocolate out of little cups. I want to get covered in chocolate all over, just like you and my granddaughter and the Fireman and Dailan Kifki."

"In that case, *supisichi!*" said the dwarf fiercely, drawing his sword again.

They started fighting, as usual, until the Superintendent separated them, using his whistle, his truncheon and his white gloves.

Once this latest torment was over, we all set off in the direction of Mister Carozo's house. It's just as well it was nice and close.

30

The house really was very near.

First you had to count out seventeen trees, go past one and a half streams, turn around, count to four, take fifteen waltz steps to the right and then fourteen tango steps to the left and... there it was.

It was a castle, really, as big as a real castle, but I thought: That dwarf isn't going to trick me again. I'm sure the castle is big on the outside and small on the inside, like the carriage.

And it was! It was very big on the outside but only little on the inside.

I wondered how so many people were going to fit inside the castle. But after all, we'd already overcome such a lot of problems I wasn't going to get alarmed now over something so trivial.

Mister Carozo made me and Granddad go in first. We ducked down and managed to crawl through the door quite comfortably.

As soon as we had passed over the threshold, we heard a terrible sobbing behind us: it was Dailan Kifki, who was heartbroken because he *really* wasn't going to fit inside. And he had noticed the divine smell of chocolate coming from the palace kitchen.

He cried so much and so excellently that I'm sure every single stamp in the Gulubú Post Office must have come unstuck.

I decided to ignore him and let him cry, which is what we usually do with badly brought up cry-babies, and as many of us as could fit made our way into the living room of Mister Dwarf's castle. In other words, me and Granddad and one or two others.

It's hard for me to describe how lovely that room was. One thing I can tell you: it wasn't a room for spending time in, or sitting around or entertaining visitors. It was a room made just for staring at. It was full of windows, big and small, which didn't keep still but moved whenever you moved. The colours were constantly shifting and changing. It was like being inside a kaleidoscope.

Can you picture it?

There were no chairs or bits of furniture or anything. Only those crazy windows and, in one corner, asleep on a crystal bed, a beautiful football that certainly must have been the one that made Mister Carozo champion.

"She's asleep now," said Mister Carozo, pointing at the ball with a serious expression on his face, "but when she wakes up, she'll score a goal right away."

"And what time does she wake up?" I asked.

"Quite eventually," he replied mysteriously.

We decided to let the ball sleep in peace, and the owner of the house invited us through to the dining room where, he explained, we were being awaited by a big table covered in a very fine tablecloth, and on that tablecloth, more than eight hundred pretty little porcelain cups already containing the steaming chocolate.

We crawled through to the dining room after him.

We arranged ourselves around the table and saw that, yes, the eight hundred little cups were indeed laid out on the fine tablecloth, but... there wasn't a single drop of chocolate left!

What could have happened?

That shameless Dailan Kifki, angry at not being allowed into the palace, had found nothing better to do than to stick his trunk through the window and drink the chocolate from all the little cups, one by one.

Would you believe it?

Though I should point out in his favour that he had managed to suck out the chocolate so delicately that he hadn't broken a single cup or spilt a single drop on that very fine starched tablecloth.

We were all looking sadly, desperately at the empty little cups, when suddenly... *Ker-BLAM!* from the living room we heard the sound of breaking glass. No sooner had we turned our heads to look than in burst the football, leaping about and spinning like a mad thing.

The uproar seemed to have woken her.

The ball started jumping about on the table, and broke several of the little cups.

"*Supisichi*, she's awake," muttered Mister Carozo.

After bouncing around happily for a good while, the ball escaped out the window and Dailan Kifki started playing with her in the palace garden.

I was most surprised that Mister Carozo, who was such a grouch, would put up with such a badly behaved ball!

Anyway, the owner of the house was just about to call his mysterious, invisible servants to replace the broken cups and prepare more chocolate, when...

I'd almost rather not remember what happened next.

It makes my hair stand on end.

31

All of a sudden, the whole castle trembled. The ground shook, paint from the roof rained down on our heads, and a hellish noise came from the living room:

Crish crash bang blam-blata-ka-blooooommmm!

"*Supisichi*, an earthquake!" we all said at once: Mister Carozo and Granddad and I, grabbing each other's hands, terrified.

However, I did think it strange that there should be an earthquake in Gulubú, since I hadn't seen a single mountain anywhere, let alone a volcano.

The three of us squeezed our eyes shut and covered our ears, certain that Dailan Kifki must have destroyed some part of the castle while playing with that football.

"I'm sure it's that elephant!" Mister Carozo roared like a lion cub.

"Let's not jump to conclusions!" I said.

"That elephant should be locked up in a school for the rest of his life!" yelled Granddad.

"I'm sure it wasn't him," I said, trying to defend poor Dailan Kifki.

"Oh no?" replied the dwarf, green with rage. "I'll bet my football it was him!"

"Done," I replied, calmly.

"*Supisichi*," added Mister Carozo. "If Dailan Kifki is innocent, you get to keep the football, with her bed and everything."

"I will."

I looked out the window and saw Dailan Kifki playing a nice, calm game of golf, pushing the ball with his trunk till she fell into an anthill.

"Look over here," I said to Mister Carozo.

I picked him up so he could see.

"So what was all that commotion?" asked Mister Carozo, intrigued.

"I don't know, but it's quite clear that Dailan Kifki isn't to blame. Which means I've won the football."

"Just a moment," said Mister Carozo, who was already regretting having bet his precious ball. "This needs to be investigated by a proper detective. You don't get the ball till we've made quite sure it really wasn't Dailan Kifki who was behind this catastrophe."

"But Mister Carozo, first we need to know what this famous catastrophe actually was! We heard the crash but so far we haven't moved from here to find out what in *sampiolin* happened," I said nervously. (Some of the dwarf's vocabulary was catching.)

"If we're to find out what happened," he replied, stubborn as ever, "we need a detective. A proper one with a magnifying glass and a pipe and everything."

"But what do we need a detective for if we can see with our own eyes? That noise, the catastrophe—it happened somewhere very near here. Probably inside the house, Mister Carozo."

But do you think the dwarf gave in?

Nope.

He didn't even bother going over to where the catastrophe had taken place. And he wouldn't let me go, either. Instead he insisted, grumbled and stamped his feet, calling for a detective with a magnifying glass and a pipe and everything.

Then we heard an ironic little laugh behind us...

Can you guess who it was?

Just imagine!

32

We turned around and our jaws dropped—there was Granddad perfectly disguised as a detective, with a little checked cloak and cap, a magnifying glass, pipe and sideburns.

"I've been a qualified detective my whole life," said Granddad with a condescending look on his face, as he polished the pipe on his sleeve.

"I'm delighted to hear it," replied Mister Carozo, shaking his hand.

And right then and there he hired him to carry out his investigation.

"All suspicions fall on the accused, Dailan Kifki!" cried Mister Dwarf.

"Not so fast," Granddad replied calmly. "The guilty party might be the football."

"No, sir! The football is playing nice and calmly in the garden!"

"Allow me to examine this football," insisted Granddad, the pipe between his teeth.

I leant out the window and asked Dailan Kifki to hand me the ball, which he did most obediently.

Granddad examined it from all angles with his magnifying glass and muttered:

"Let's wait for the police to show up and take this football away as a suspect."

"I will absolutely not permit that, by *sampiolín!*" roared the dwarf.

But Granddad interrupted him, very calmly, and said:

"We shall proceed with the investigation. First we need to know where the whole commotion came from and what physical damage has taken place."

"I think the noise came from the living room," I said. "All the little cups in here are still in one piece."

"Then let us go through to the living room," said Granddad calmly, pointing the way with his pipe.

And off the three of us went, hand in hand.

There was no longer a living room.

There was only a pile of shattered fragments of glass in every colour. There was no trace left of the football's glass crib. Nor of the frames of those lovely crazy windows that moved like a kaleidoscope.

The three of us fell silent, looking down at the toes of our shoes.

I felt a big tear escaping. It rolled down my cheek and burst with a *clink* against the broken glass that carpeted the floor.

Mister Carozo was quite still, his hat in his hand and his head bowed.

I stroked him a bit to comfort him, because I could easily imagine just how sad he must have been feeling.

Such a beautiful living room. One of a kind.

"Who was it?" he whimpered. "Who broke my lovely little living room? Who did it?"

"Sir," said Granddad, putting a hand on his shoulder, "this is one of the greatest mysteries in the history of Gulubú. But we will solve it, with the help of my pipe, my magnifying glass, and my extraordinary intelligence."

Granddad was becoming more modest every day.

He took a little notebook from the back pocket of his big golf trousers and wrote:

THE CASE OF THE DISAPPEARING ROOM

"The first thing we have to do," he said next, putting the notebook away again, "is question everyone who is in the vicinity of the house."

"But we'll never finish that, Granddad! There are, like, eight hundred thousand people!"

"And somewhere among them," said Granddad, sucking on his pipe, "is the guilty party."

We went out into the garden, where our whole retinue was camped out under the trees in the clover.

Everybody was behaving all absent-minded and innocent, which looked very suspicious if you ask me.

Granddad climbed up onto a tree trunk and, standing in front of his audience, he said in a big, calm voice:

"A terrible calamity has just taken place in this castle."

"What calamity?" everyone asked, looking all innocent again, even though it was right there under their noses: the living room smashed into little pieces.

"Certain criminal elements have destroyed Mister Carozo's living room," said Granddad.

"Oooooh, have they really?" everyone said, as though they hadn't noticed.

"We didn't see a thing," said one ambassador, who I'm sure was a shameless liar.

"And you didn't hear the noise either?" asked Granddad.

"No," said the Superintendent, "because we were all singing *zambas.*"

"I would most earnestly entreat you," said Granddad, "to assist me in this investigation, so that we might avoid the injustice of condemning an innocent man."

"Of course, of course. We're at your service," everyone said.

"I would ask you then to move a bit farther off," said Granddad, "and keep a bit of distance from the site of the catastrophe, because I'm going to be using my magnifying glass to study the marks on the ground."

Everyone moved back in silence, while Granddad got down on his hands and knees and set about studying the ground with his powerful English magnifying glass.

Mister Carozo stood with me and cried, covering his eyes with my pinafore.

33

Poor Mister Carozo!

I stroked the little dwarf's head and tried to console him.

"Don't worry yourself, Mister Carozo. Between us we'll be able to put your living room back together."

"And till then, where's the football going to sleep?" he asked, hiccuping inconsolably.

"She can sleep at the foot of your bed, Mister Carozo."

"No, she doesn't like that. In the middle of the night she has bad dreams, and then she jumps on my bed and startles me."

"Don't upset yourself. Granddad will discover the guilty party, and he'll make him rebuild the room as a punishment."

"My lovely little room with its crazy windows in every colour..."

In order to distract him, I invited him into the kitchen to prepare some yummy oats soup for Dailan Kifki.

I thought it strange that I hadn't seen a single servant anywhere in the castle, or a single cook in the kitchen.

"You can't see them, but I've got lots," the dwarf explained.

I had to cook on my knees because the kitchen was so small.

When we went out to take the soup to Dailan Kifki, Granddad was crawling around the ruined living room, sniffing at the floor like a bloodhound and squinting at it through his magnifying glass.

"An ant," said Granddad, and made a note in his little notebook.

"A cockroach wearing a wig," said Granddad, making a note of this suspicious discovery, too.

"An embarrassed-looking earthworm." And he made another note.

This is never going to end! I thought to myself, alarmed.

All of a sudden, Granddad stopped and buried his nose in the ground.

He looked with his magnifying glass, and looked again. He compared what he was looking at with the ant, the cockroach and the worm. He got out a ruler and a pair of compasses and took a careful measurement of whatever he was looking at, made another note in his notebook, then came over and whispered in my ear:

"I think I've got it."

"The culprit, Granddad?"

"Aha!"

"And it isn't Dailan Kifki, is it?"

"We'll see about that very soon," he said, calmly. "I've found a footprint with a circumference of one centimetre in diameter. Now we just need to measure Dailan Kifki's feet. If they're the same size, he's certainly the guilty party. There are many identical tracks."

"I think Dailan Kifki's feet are a bit bigger than that, Granddad."

"That's what I've got to check with my ruler and compasses. Bring me the accused at once!"

I went to fetch Dailan Kifki, who had finished his soup, and led him by the ear to appear before the detective.

"Very good," said Granddad. "Let us proceed to the chrono-logical, numismatical, peripatetical investigation of the finger-prints of this proboscidean, in a philatelical comparison with the parallelepipedical and symptomatical tracks found in the neighbouring terrain."

Which must have meant he was going to see if Dailan Kifki's feet matched the prints he'd found in the mud.

Granddad took out his little notebook and checked the measurements of the footprints: one centimetre.

Then he took his ruler and compasses and, with my help, bent one of Dailan Kifki's legs and carefully measured the sole of his foot.

"Forty-eight centimetres, fifteen millimetres," said Granddad, and made a note in his notebook.

"You see?" I said. "They aren't his footprints."

"Just to be sure, let's test them out in practice."

And he positioned Dailan Kifki's foot over one of the small holes he had discovered in the ground.

"There are precisely forty-seven centimetres and fifteen millimetres to spare," he said. "Therefore these footprints do not belong to the accused."

I gave a sigh of relief.

The footprints were small round holes, arranged regularly.

Those weren't made by shoes, I thought to myself, or by a skateboard, or by chickens.

"These footprints are very odd," I said to Granddad. "If you ask me, they're the prints of an animal with only one foot."

"Nonsense!" he said. "Have you ever seen an animal with only one foot?"

"Well, let me think..."—and I put my finger to my forehead and started to think—"Snails don't have any, flies have several—but anyway why would they bother walking if they can fly... Tables do have legs, but they aren't animals..."

"That's it!" Granddad interrupted me. "You're right, the guilty party might have one or more feet but not be an animal at all!"

"Just one foot..." My head hurt from so much thinking. Then... "I've got it, Granddad!" I cried suddenly, overjoyed. "An umbrella!"

"That's it!" cried Granddad, hugging me, his eyes filling with tears. "These are umbrella footprints! I suspected it all along!"

"But Granddad," I said, trying to calm him down, "you aren't telling me that a poor umbrella could have caused such an earthquake?"

"Oh no?" replied Granddad mysteriously.

And he walked over to where the busybodies were, and the dignitaries, and the neighbours, and all the people drinking *mate* with perfectly innocent expressions on their faces.

But he stopped halfway, took out his little notebook, and wrote:

THE CASE OF THE KILLER UMBRELLA

34

Granddad climbed up onto a rock, rang the bell *clang clang*, and shushed emphatically several times, until he had managed to get everyone impressively quiet.

Then he said:

"Children!"

"Present..." everybody replied, filled with fear, and with terror, scares and afraidness.

"Following my extensive investigations," said Granddad, "and thanks to my magnifying glass and my pipe, I have been able to discover that the guilty party, or the main accomplice of this immense catastrophe, has only one foot, and therefore is an umbrella."

A murmur of amazement came from the crowd.

"I ask anyone present who is in possession of an umbrella," he went on, "to come forward at once and present themselves at this police station."

And then he stopped, peering down at them like some kind of big-shot and waiting for the guilty umbrella to show its face.

Nothing.

Nobody moved.

"This is your last chance," Granddad said severely. "I would advise any umbrella that is among you, whether living or dead, wet or dry, to show itself at once."

And then we heard a shrill voice protesting:

"Why are you going after a poor, defenceless umbrella, when everybody knows that pesky elephant is the guilty one?"

I got furious when I heard such slander, but that was nothing compared to Dailan Kifki's reaction. He shook his ears and trunk as though he were about to eat my Auntie Clodomira all up.

Because she was the person who had spoken, getting quite indignant and waving her umbrella as she did.

She immediately began to argue with Granddad, and everyone started to make comments and argue and take sides and bet on one or the other.

There was such a commotion that nobody realised my auntie was twirling the very object everyone was looking for: her umbrella. The famous umbrella she was never separated from, not even leaving it in the umbrella-stand when she went to bed.

In the middle of the fight, Granddad spotted it, and said:

"But how can you dare to accuse this poor innocent elephant when you're holding the true culprit in your very hand for all to see: Your Umbrella!"

"What?... Who says?... But how?... For whom?..." stammered my Auntie Clodomira, staring at her umbrella and squinting cross-eyed with amazement, since with all the arguing even she hadn't realised she was holding it.

"What do you want with my poor umbrella who wouldn't hurt a fly?" whimpered my aunt at last.

"We must see if its footprints match the ones I've made a note of in my notebook!" bellowed Granddad, snatching the umbrella away from her.

I don't have to tell you that at this point my aunt fainted.

While one of the Ambassadors tried to get her out of the plant pot she'd fallen into, Granddad measured and re-measured the foot of the umbrella, which as everybody knows is called a *ferrule*, and compared it, magnifying glass in hand, with the footprints.

Soon afterwards, my Auntie Clodomira came to again, only to faint again when Granddad said solemnly:

"I hereby declare that this umbrella is, if not actually the culprit, certainly highly suspicious."

The crowd, looking askance at my Auntie Clodomira, said:

"Oooooooooooooooh!"

I went over to Granddad and said:

"Granddad, have you ever seen an umbrella that could walk around on its own, or smash up a living room on its own?"

"That's because it didn't do it alone," said Granddad. "It was in your aunt's hand, as it always is."

"That's not possible," I said. "Why would she want to smash up Mister Carozo's living room?"

"We shall question her," said Granddad.

And off he went to question my Auntie Clodomira.

When she saw him walking towards her, looking so determined, my aunt got into a real dither, saying:

"Itwasntme, itwasntme, itwasntme, itwasntme..."

But it wasn't long before, beset by remorse, she confessed to everything.

And I, following my granddad's orders, took notes in shorthand of my aunt's confession.

My Aunt's Confession is so important it deserves a chapter to itself.

If you read it, you'll learn absolutely all of truthfullest truth from the mouth of the real culprit.

I didn't change a single comma of the confession, but it's possible there might be a few words missing because there was a sparrow pecking at the piece of paper while I was making my notes and, as far as I can tell, there were certain words it particularly liked, even if they were written in shorthand.

And the ones it liked, it pecked out and took away with it.

That was how, the next day, I saw a nest full of pencil scribblings...

But that has nothing to do with the bloodcurdling crime story I was just telling you.

Sorry about that.

35

My Auntie Clodomira's Confession

It wasn't me, it wasn't me, it wasn't me...

Well, yes, all right, it was me. But I didn't do it on purpose!

You all know very well, gentlemen, that I'm not a bad person, or a nasty person or a person who breaks things. On the contrary, I'm considerate and obliging, and wasn't I brewing up mate for all of you just a week ago? What happened was, everybody wanted to get into the house of Mister Dwarf Carozo Somethingorother.

Isn't that true? Yes—everybody! Everyone was curious, and so was I, gentlemen of the jury. I was desperate to go in and have a nose around, and why not? Where's the harm in that? I also wanted—just like everyone else—to taste the hot chocolate in pretty little porcelain cups. But as the house was so small, we ended up with only Granddad and my niece getting in, and no one else. But when I smelt that hot chocolate smell, I did so want to look in a little—only just a little. And so I peered through the door to the living room, and since the doorway was so narrow, I ended up getting stuck there, unable either to go in or out. Not in, or out! Of course it's true: I am a bit fat, almost as fat as that elephant or as four letterboxes tied together with a piece of twine. And so I pushed a little, using my umbrella as a crowbar, and... Crash bang clang Ker-BLAM! The door came down and the rest of the room with it, including that lovely big window with glass in every colour. But I can assure you my umbrella is innocent! He didn't even want to try the chocolate! And now that I've confessed everything, Mister Detective, you can arrest me and...

(At this point my aunt's tears were flowing so fast that they wiped away the rest of the confession and flooded the garden.)

36

"What punishment does she deserve, *too-loora-loora-lay?*" asked Mister Dwarf Carozo.

"Let me think," said Granddad, with his finger on his forehead.

Nobody knew how she ought to be punished. Not until Mister Carozo himself had a brilliant idea:

"Make her rebuild my castle living room!"

"But how am I supposed to rebuild it when I'm not a builder?" protested my desperate Auntie Clodomira.

"So make it out of wood instead, *too-loora-loora-lay,*" sang Mister Carozo.

"But I'm not a carpenter," said my aunt, in the middle of an attack of hiccups.

"So make it out of leather then, *too-loora-loora-lay,*" insisted Mister Carozo.

"But I'm not a leatherworker!" said my aunt.

"So make it out of sweet meringue, *too-loora-loora-lay,*" insisted Mister Carozo.

And then my aunt said nothing.

Because cooking... well, that was something she *did* know how to do. And especially making meringues, sponge cakes, puff pastries and tarts with flourishes of cream and chopped walnuts.

"Very well, then," said my aunt, heading for the kitchen with a determined look on her face.

But since we were scared she'd break the kitchen, too, we took several heaters and all the ingredients out into the garden.

And so like that, bit by bit, with a great deal of patience and skill, my Auntie Clodomira began to rebuild the room, all the while using her umbrella to shoo away the busybodies who kept wanting to taste it.

She prepared huge bricks of sponge cake, and used them to put up the walls.

It goes without saying that she joined the bricks together using thick, sticky *dulce de leche*.

The walls were perfect, and everyone applauded.

"Don't applaud yet," said my aunt. "There's still a lot to be done."

And she started to prepare the famous windows, using candies of every colour. They were almost identical to the windows that had been there before.

Then she put on the roof. Made of chocolate, naturally.

At that point the military authorities from our expedition had to step in, to prevent all the people there from eating it.

When she was done with the roofing, everyone applauded again.

My aunt waved her skirt at them and said:

"No, no, don't applaud yet. There's still a lot to be done." And she started to paint the walls with the whitest sugar.

Again everyone applauded, but my aunt warned them:

"Don't applaud yet. It still needs the finishing touches."

And she dotted the newly whitened walls artistically with coloured sweets.

And now, yes, now my Auntie Clodomira, wiping her brow with her apron and absolutely exhausted, received all the great applause from the crowd, beaming with delight.

Mister Carozo, glad to have his living room back, asked me to pick him up so he could give my aunt a kiss.

And so the Case of the Disappearing Room and the Killer Umbrella ended happily for everybody.

And I had won Mister Carozo's football, because Dailan Kifki was innocent.

Ha ha ha.

37

But I soon had to stop laughing when I saw Mister Carozo heading over very calmly to fetch his sleepy football to put her back into his little living room.

"Just one moment, Mister Carozo!" I called out to him.

"What's the matter?" he replied, playing dumb.

"I'm very sorry to tell you," I answered, "that the ball you're carrying is no longer yours but mine, completely mine and so very much mine."

"*Supisichi*," he answered. "This ball is mine, completely mine and so very much mine and has been for a hundred and eighty-five years."

"No, sir. Maybe because you're a dwarf you have a very short memory, but let me remind you, sir, that you bet me that football, sir, and I won it from you fair and square, sir."

"Me?" he asked, pretending to be shocked. "Me, bet my precious football? Me? Do my ears deceive me?"

I picked him up again, pushed aside his hat, lifted the hair of his sideburns a bit and yelled in his ear:

"Yes, sir, you bet me the football and you lost so I'm taking her away with *me*!"

"And what were we playing when I bet her?" he asked me, his eyes wide. "Were we playing ludo, hopscotch, dominoes, body-part tag, jacks?"

"No, sir," I said, this time lifting the sideburn from his other ear, "you bet me because you thought Dailan Kifki was the person who murdered your living room, and the police investigation has shown that the poor creature was innocent."

"Oh, by *sampiolin*," he replied impatiently. "Put me down, I have a lot to do."

"No, sir, there's no way I'm putting you down," I answered, still holding him up in the air, even though he was kicking his feet like crazy, his slippers spinning. I held him a bit farther away from me, but I did not put him back on the ground.

"The football is mine, so very much mine!" I insisted.

"Oh, and what do I care," he said, at last. "Take your football. The Forest of Gulubú is full of footballs just as clever as that one."

And so I put him down on the ground, and he ran into the house and quickly came back out with the football in his arms.

He gave her to me. But very unwillingly.

38

I t seemed that our problems were over, along with our muddles, our plans, turnarounds, disasters and all the chocolate in those little cups.

It seemed we were at last going to be setting off back to Ituzaingó station, and from there back home.

Everyone was making preparations: they were buffing their top hats with their sleeves, buttoning up their waistcoats, blowing the dirt off their shoes, combing their hair with their fingers, and so on.

Granddad made us line up in front of Mister Carozo, and we took it in turns to shake his hand and say, "Thank you very much for your hospitality."

The owner of the house seemed quite downhearted at our departure, and as he combed his beard with his little finger he muttered thoughtfully:

"*Supisichisupisichisupisichi...*"

It was obvious that the moment we left he was going to start crying.

Dailan Kifki was very sad, too. He had loved it in the Forest of Gulubú, which must surely have reminded him of his home in Africa.

But really, we couldn't stay for ever.

No sooner had we taken our first few steps away than my Auntie Clodomira shouted:

"Halt! Eyes... *right!*"

And we all turned towards the work she had created—which by then was covered in flies and bees—with one final admiring glance.

We were just about ready to go on our way, with Mister Carozo waving us goodbye with a handkerchief much bigger than he was, bathed in tears.

I had to promise him we would be back.

He threw his arms around my knees, drying his eyes and his sideburns on my pinafore.

I had to tickle the back of his neck.

When he had calmed down a little, we began our retreat.

Dailan Kifki was at the head of the retinue, and I was behind him, my arms around the sleepy football, who was snoring away happily.

Following us in procession came: my family, the Fireman, the Captain, the Ambassadors, the Mini-Secretary, the Mayor and all the other characters you know about already. And behind them, the neighbours, busybodies, ice-cream sellers, altar boys and a dog with two tails.

It was beginning to get dark, and a dreadful question occurred to me. Where were we going? Because the Forest of Gulubú is very large.

I went over to Granddad and asked him in a whisper:

"Granddad, where are we going?"

"What do you mean, where are we going?" he replied. "To Ituzaingó station."

"Yes, I know that, but did you ask Mister Carozo where it is?"

"No, I thought you knew the way," said Granddad.

"I haven't the faintest idea, Granddad," I said, upset.

"Don't worry, I've got a compass in my pocket."

"What use is a compass if we don't know if the station is to the north or to the south, to the east or on the coast?" I asked in alarm.

My brother Roberto overheard the conversation and said: "We're toast."

Granddad stopped the retinue and said we would need to send a messenger to Mister Carozo's house to ask him to explain the way.

Then my brother Roberto opened his mouth, and instead of saying "We're toast," as usual, he said:

"I've got an idea."

And he was right—he did.

"There's only one person," he said, "who can find his way in the dark, and that's Dailan Kifki."

"You're crazy," I said.

"Nobody with a trunk that big ever gets lost," insisted my brother.

I didn't think one thing had anything to do with the other, but anyway...

The two of us went off to look for Dailan Kifki, who had fallen asleep beside a eucalyptus tree.

"Dailan, sweetie," I said in his ear. "Which way's the station?"

No reply.

I asked him another sixteen times. Nothing. Not a peep.

"That's not the way to ask Dailan Kifki a question," said Roberto.

"So how are you supposed to talk to him? In African?"

"I know how to do it," said Roberto.

And he approached Dailan Kifki's enormous left ear and yelled:

"Dailan-Kifki-there-are-seventeen-barrels-of-lovely-milky-oats-soup-just-waiting-for-you-at-Ituzaingó-station!"

And Dailan Kifki raced off like a mad thing! We barely had time to get to our feet and follow him. Some lost their top hats, others a shoe, some bumped into one another, others had their wigs knocked out of place.

But follow him we did, all of us singing the *San Lorenzo March*, our eyes set on the future.

We trotted along for several hours until finally, all the way off in the distance, we saw a small light and heard the whistle of the locomotives.

Dailan Kifki picked up the pace, unfolding his great ears and stretching his trunk out towards the barrels of soup.

I felt ever so bad that we'd deceived him so meanly. That kind of behaviour is really not on.

39

You're not going to believe it, but we did finally make it to Ituzaingó station. I took a good look at the signs, because I was very afraid we might have come to some *other* Ituzaingó station, the one on the Someplaceorother Railway, or in the Republic of Sanantonín.

But we hadn't.

It was written everywhere, quite clearly: The Domingo Faustino Sarmiento Railroad, in the Republic of Argentina.

So as not to tire you out too much, I'm skipping right over the part where Granddad saw the great man's name and took off his helmet and tried to make us all sing *The Anthem to President Sarmiento*.

It wasn't that we had anything against the former President. On the contrary, we love him a lot, but we just didn't have the strength to do any singing.

So Granddad sang the *Anthem* all on his own, several times.

Everyone pounced on the candy stall: they weren't too tired for that. In seconds they had ransacked it completely.

And at this point I ought to record a very sweet gesture on the part of the Fireman.

He went over to the stall, then trotted back to me, took off his lovely golden helmet, bowed low and handed me a packet of orange lozenges.

My mother, who was standing nearby, whispered to me:

"Such a gentleman, that Fireman! The moment we arrive home, you're going to have to marry him."

At that exact moment the train arrived.

Granddad ordered us to form a queue, and I got right to the front, holding on to Dailan Kifki by one ear so he wouldn't escape again.

The sleek Japanese train came to a halt, the door opened, and I said to my elephant:

"Come on, then, sweetheart, up you go, nice and slowly, first one foot, then the other..."

It was the first time Dailan Kifki had ever got on a train, and naturally he was a bit shy.

At last we made it on, and fortunately the train was almost empty.

But one lady, seeing an elephant coming into the compartment, stuck her head out the window and gave a terrible scream:

"Heeeeeeeeeeelp!"

"Sssshhh," we all hissed.

"Madam," I said, "have you never seen an adorable little animal like this before?"

"But travelling on the train with animals is forbidden!" she shouted, even more angrily.

"Oh, but he's really affectionate," I said. "If I'd wanted to get on a train with a raging lion, or a panther without a muzzle, or a crazy mouse, then yes, perhaps..."

"It's still forbidden!" she replied. "Haven't you seen in the newspapers that you're not allowed to go out with animals, in case they might have rabies?"

"But please, madam—Dailan Kifki isn't a dog. How's he going to have rabies?"

"Either you get him out of here," said the lady, "or I shall call the police."

The guard arrived.

"What's going on?" he asked.

"Nothing, nothing..." I said, trying to hide Dailan Kifki behind me.

The lady pointed her finger at me and shrieked:

"This young woman is trying to travel with an animal!"

Dailan Kifki was hiding behind me, doing his best to look as small as possible.

"Right, then, let's have a look," said the guard.

I was shaking with terror that he was going to make us all get off, when...

40

The guard saw that I was carrying... a cage! Because I forgot to tell you: since our famous disaster with Mister Carozo's living room had destroyed the crystal house where the football lived, he'd put her into a cage for me so she could sleep and travel more comfortably.

Naturally, the guard's attention was caught by the cage and, distracted by the commotion everyone was making, he saw nothing else.

"Didn't you know you aren't allowed to board a train carrying an animal, even if it's in a cage?" he said.

"But I'm not carrying an animal in this cage, Mister Guard."

"You aren't going to try and make me believe that you're travelling with a cage full of nothing, miss?"

"Not full of nothing, sir, no. This is the cage where the famous Football sleeps."

(I said it with a capital letter, to sound more impressive.)

"Well, you don't say..." said the guard, very impressed, scratching under his cap. It turned out he was a great football fan.

So my brother Roberto and I invented a whole heap of stories of famous matches, famous players, famous goals, etc.

All the football chatter meant the train wasn't leaving, of course, and the passengers were starting to protest, though actually not all that much since they were all quite used to our trains running about as slow as a tortoise. (With apologies to my tortoise friends who I know are very serious people indeed.)

And the guard went on nattering away, looking again and again at the ball between the golden bars of her little cage.

At that moment I could feel that pesky Dailan Kifki slipping and sliding and shifting about very slowly behind me. I tried to hide him, blocking the sight of him with my skirt and chatting to the guard even more animatedly.

Until a moment later—out the corner of my eye what did I see but the shameless creature sitting in one of the train seats, right in front of the moaning lady!

You can imagine the state of my nerves.

So Dailan Kifki settled himself into the seat, all twisted up and with his feet squeezed in towards him. I don't know how he did it, but he managed to fit pretty well, with only a few tons of him spilling out through the window and over into the aisle.

Fortunately at this point the lady was reading her newspaper so she didn't notice him.

I asked the guard if he could please get the train on its way soon, thinking, Well, if Dailan Kifki keeps nice and still, and the lady in front goes on reading her newspaper, we might just make it to Miserere Square safely.

Nope.

Dailan Kifki had started peering at the comic strips on the back page of the lady's newspaper. But as his eyesight wasn't all that great for reading, he had to lean forward a little, and then a little more, until he had his trunk right up against the paper and was just about to lose his balance...

I was terrified he'd fall on top of the lady. So I tried to hurry the guide to hurry the engine driver to hurry the signalman to hurry the crossing-keeper to hurry the cow who was crossing the tracks so that the train could get on its way once and for all.

And just when everyone had finished hurrying everyone else, and the guard was blowing on his whistle and waving his green handkerchief and the train was about to pull out of the station... *Ker-BLAM!*

What do you think happened?

Dailan Kifki fell on the lady!

She gave a horrible shriek:

"Help! S.O.S.! Murderers! Earthquake! Disaster!"

A completely unnecessary fuss, because Dailan hadn't fallen on her *completely*, of course, only his head.

Now, naturally, his head, including his ears and trunk, does weigh a good number of kilos, but still there was no reason for quite so much screaming.

I tried to lift Dailan Kifki's head from her lap. I tried really, really hard. Roberto helped me, and the guard helped me, and the Ambassadors helped me, and so did Auntie Clodomira.

You won't believe it, but between all of us we still weren't able to lift Dailan Kifki's huge head. It was like he was glued to the lady's knees.

At this point the ticket inspector arrived, fiddling very seriously with his little ticket-punching machine.

"What's going on?" he asked.

"Nothing, nothing, Mister Inspector!" we all said in chorus, blocking his view of the accident with our bodies while my dad put his hand over the lady's mouth.

And we all kept struggling to lift Dailan Kifki's head.

Nothing.

Hup! Hup! *Hup*...

Still nothing.

He was glued to the lady's knees.

Shaking him made no difference, nor did tickling him, nor did flicking his ears as hard as we could.

Do you know what the problem was?

Dailan Kifki had fallen asleep! Now we really were totally, completely, utterly toast.

"I'm afraid you're just going to have to be a bit patient, madam," I said to the noisy passenger. "The poor thing is a very deep sleeper."

Then I lifted one of Dailan Kifki's ears, and said into it:

"Let's eat some lovely oats soup..."

At which point he woke up, yawned a little, and between us we managed to settle him back into his seat.

My father had managed to gag the lady with his handkerchief and necktie.

The inspector, who had been in conversation with the guard, came over to me and said:

"I'm sorry, miss. We've given you a special permit to travel with your football, but there is simply no way we can authorise your being on here with an elephant. I'm sorry, but rules are rules."

Which was how our entire retinue, who had only just managed to settle ourselves into the compartment and had only just finished arguing over the windows, had to get back off the train, pushing a half-asleep Dailan Kifki off with us.

There we were again, at midnight, taking up the whole platform of Ituzaingó station.

41

Sometimes I just don't get people. For example: everyone's perfectly used to being shoved around on buses and trains and subways, shoved and squeezed and getting their hair mussed up and being pulled this way and that. And no one complains. But oh, the second they realise that it's an *elephant* shoving them, well then, *Ker-BLAM!* You wouldn't believe the noise they make!

Like that blessed lady who went off on her train very happily, leaving all the rest of us dejected, starving, cold and tired on Ituzaingó station.

You can't imagine how sadly Dailan Kifki watched the departing train. Naturally, he immediately started to cry. And naturally, soon enough the Ituzaingó postmaster showed up. He had been working late, and apparently no sooner had he managed to get the stamps back in order than the elephant's tearful explosion had made the building shake so much that they were all soon flying about again like confetti. The Superintendent pretended to start legal proceedings against us, and the postmaster was a bit happier after that.

"It's simply not possible," I said to them all, "that having successfully completed the most astronautically phantasmagorical bit of the expedition, we're now going to be stuck at anchor here in this station for ever. We have to find some quick, simple way of getting home."

"Why don't we walk?" asked my mum.

"It's too far, we're tired," grumbled the others between yawns.

"What if we put the wings back on Dailan Kifki?" suggested my brother Roberto.

"Then he'll escape again," I said.

"No," Roberto went on, "listen. We tie him to a very long piece of twine, so that way we can't lose him even if he's flying all over the sky."

But the person with the smartest idea was Granddad.

"Attention!" he said. "What we need to do is wait for a cargo train to come past, and we put Dailan Kifki in with the cows. Nobody will see much difference between a cow and an elephant while it's still dark."

"Yes, that is a very good idea," I said. "But where will we travel? We can't go in with the cows, too."

"We'll take a bus!" said Dad.

"Honestly," I replied, "do you really think I'm ever likely to let Dailan Kifki travel all on his own?"

"But he'll be with the cows," Dad insisted. "They'll take care of him. Cows are really affectionate."

"No, sir," I said, "there's absolutely no way I'm letting him travel alone in a dark railway wagon with some cows we don't know anything about and who we've never met before."

And then my Auntie Clodomira said:

"Why don't you go with him in the cattle wagon, then?"

"Because I'm not a cow, Auntie!"

And on the argument went, for quite some time.

Fortunately no cargo trains came by.

After we'd done enough arguing, we decided to try thinking. So we all put our fingers to our foreheads and the whole line

of us circled up and down the platform. We had turned into a
kind of merry-go-round.

We went up and down thinking and re-thinking in silence,
when suddenly... do you know who showed up?

Just imagine!

Can you guess?

42

Mister Dwarf Carozo Minujín.

"But what are you doing here, Mister Carozo? We thought you'd be asleep at this time."

"Yes, I was sleeping," he replied.

He opened his frock coat, and underneath it he was wearing a fustian nightshirt. He lifted his hat, and underneath that he had another cap, this one knitted and with a pompom at the end. He took off one of his slippers and underneath he was wearing another, made of wool.

"I was sleeping," he said, "but suddenly... Waaaaaahhhhh!"

And he started to cry like a little madman.

(I don't want to tire you out, so I'll skip over the inevitable bit where the postmaster showed up, crimson with rage because of the new tearful explosion that had shaken his office and his philatelical stamps all over again.)

"What's happened, Mister Carozo?" I asked.

"Pick me up and I'll tell you," he said, like a spoilt brat.

So I picked him up, walked him about a bit, waiting for his hiccups to pass, and finally he told me:

"I was asleep and I had a dream about my football. I missed her so much, I came running here to see whether you all... still... *supisichi*..."

And what with all his crying and his hiccuping, he couldn't say any more.

I consoled him as best I could, though I could tell he was only sobbing so much because he was trying his luck to see if I'd give him his ball back.

"Mister Carozo," I said, "here's your football in her little cage, but I'm sure you know: *Taking back something you've given a friend, is a sure-fire way for a friendship to end.*"

He immediately threw his arms around the cage, hugging it tightly—as if I'd never won it fair and square in the first place.

His crying and his sleepiness disappeared and he became instantly delighted.

Having stared at his football for a good long while, he finally looked at all of us.

"And what the *supisichi* are you all doing here in the station?" he asked at last.

We told him about all the misfortunes that had befallen us.

"Ah," said Mister Carozo. "So what the *supisichi* are you going to do now?"

"Well, that was just what we were thinking about when you arrived," I replied.

"So that means I've got to think now, too?"

"If it's not too much trouble," I said.

"Very well then, I will have a think, though I really am rather sleepy."

Mister Carozo frowned, put his finger to his forehead and took three little steps around to join the queue of thinking people.

We spent a long while like that, in silence, going round our merry-go-round of thoughts, when suddenly Mister Carozo stepped away from the line and said:

"That's it, I've done my thinking."

"And what have you thought, what have you thought?" we all asked, dying of curiosity. We crouched down around Mister Carozo, who said:

"Dailan Kifki cannot travel by train because he's an elephant, right?"

"Right."

"Well then," the dwarf went on, "it's very simple. We have to disguise him so nobody realises he's an elephant."

You see how clever Mister Carozo is? Such a simple idea, and it hadn't occurred to any of us, in spite of our fingers and eyebrows being quite numb from so much thinking.

"Very well, then, Mister Carozo," I said. "So what should we disguise him as, *too-loora-loora-lay?*"

"Elephants are really big, right?" replied Mister Carozo. "So we have to disguise him as something really tiny so nobody notices how big he is."

Once again the crowd murmured their amazement at such vast intelligence in such a small gentleman.

I asked again:

"So what should we disguise him as, *too-loora-loora-lay?*"

"As something terribly small!"

And we all went back into our merry-go-round of thoughts, fingers back on our foreheads, frowning and muttering:

"Something terribly small... something terribly small... something terribly small..."

"That's it!" said Mister Carozo at last. "A butterfly! He'll be very good at pretending that because he used to be a flying elephant."

My brother Roberto said:

"We're toast."

"But why?" we all asked.

"Because a butterfly is an animal," Roberto answered, "so we'll just end up having the same problem: you aren't allowed to travel with animals."

"A butterfly isn't an animal, it's a creepy-crawly," I said, "just a little creepy-crawly that could easily have come in through the window without buying a ticket."

"Yes, but a butterfly as fat as Dailan Kifki will arouse too much suspicion," Roberto insisted, being a big old spoilsport as usual.

"And so what should we disguise him as, *too-loora-loora-lay?*" I asked once again.

"There is one solution," said Roberto. I have no idea how he was able to think so much at this time of night.

"So what's the solution?"

"We have to disguise Dailan Kifki as a person, not a creepy-crawly or an animal."

Such intelligence astounded us.

My brother Roberto thanked us modestly, his eyes lowered, as the crowd went wild with applause.

43

Roberto became the centre of everybody's attention. Within a few moments he had lost all his modesty and he was talking like an old politician, signing autographs and looking at us over his shoulder. He gave a kind of speech, in which he said two things:

First: so that the elephant wasn't seen by the guard or the train passengers, we would have to disguise him as an actual passenger himself.

Second...

I don't actually remember what bit of nonsense he said after that.

"And how do we disguise him, then, *too-loora-loora-lay?*" I insisted.

"That's what we have to think about," everyone said, and they went back to their frowning and putting their fingers to their foreheads and walking in their merry-go-round formation.

Everybody seemed excited at the idea of the whole thinking game, but frankly I was a bit bored with it. So I clapped my hands and made them break ranks.

"Enough thinking!" I ordered them. "Now it's time to act: we have to disguise Dailan Kifki as a train passenger."

"And what kind of outfit does a train passenger wear?" asked my mother, who was as fast asleep as a table.

"One with lapels and buttons... and sleeves, Mum."

"But the things we're wearing are never going to fit Dailan Kifki!" everyone protested, though really out of complete stinginess, because they just didn't want to lend the poor animal any of their own clothes.

"Come on now, don't be selfish," I said. "Start giving him any items of clothing you've got that aren't absolutely essential. Even if they're small we can join them up. We can add some buttons and sew it all together, one piece at a time."

And do you know what they all did?

They clung like crazy to their overcoats and their suits and their top hats and their wallets.

And so I took off my pinafore.

And so they were all embarrassed.

And so, slowly, bit by bit, one of them donated a hat, another a button. That man over there gave a sock, another gave a tie, someone very stingy gave a little bottle-top, my aunt a small hankie.

Everyone lined up and, in complete silence, threw their donations at Dailan Kifki's feet.

I soon found myself standing beside a pretty decent pile of clothes. But how would we arrange them so they could be used as a disguise for Dailan Kifki?

My mother and Auntie Clodomira tried to join together several overcoats with safety pins and put them over him like a huge cloak. But Dailan Kifki just looked like a mountain in disguise, and not a train passenger.

We also put several hats on him, one on top of the other... Useless.

As for me, I tried just throwing all the clothes on top of his back and ears, all higgledy-piggledy... Then I took a few steps back to see how he looked.

A complete mess.

The most disheartening thing of all was that he looked just as much an elephant as ever.

And so, practically in tears, I returned everybody's clothes, and thanked them.

Naturally they all started fighting, pushing and shoving and arguing over the clothes.

To make matters worse, Mister Carozo, who seemed to be the only sensible person in the retinue, had disappeared.

And to cap it all, the postmaster showed up to complain that with all the commotion of people taking off bits of clothing, all the stamps had come unstuck again.

Oh, give me patience!

We were just about ready to give up and set off on foot when some painters arrived with their paint-spattered overalls, ladders, brushes and tubs of paint.

They began to daub the station walls with big letters that said HOORAY FOR! and DOWN WITH!

We looked at them vaguely, since we had nothing better to do now than yawn and despair.

And then, as I looked at them, and looked at them again, my little bulb suddenly lit up.

I had THE IDEA.

Why not paint a train passenger costume on Dailan Kifki?

Aren't there circuses where they paint their elephants?

Why not?

Eh?

I'm not very good at painting, but you know, in an emergency...

I didn't say anything to anyone, because I was sure my brother Roberto would just answer:

"We're toast."

So I approached the painters on tiptoe.

"Good evening," I said.

They took off their little newspaper hats.

"Would you be so kind as to lend me a bit of paint and a thick paintbrush?"

"Certainly," they said. "But what are you going to be painting at this time of night?"

I didn't tell them I was planning to paint an elephant, as they would think I was crazy.

One of the painters looked me up and down, scratching his paper hat, and finally asked:

"Are you with all those strange people?"

"Actually, those people are very important," I replied.

As it was very dark and very crowded, it wasn't easy to make out Dailan Kifki, but the painter could see there was definitely something very big there indeed.

"And that kind of mountain thing over there... what's that?"

"What mountain?" I asked, acting all absent-minded.

"That mountain," the painter insisted.

"A mountain?" I replied, pretending to squint towards it. "Oh, I don't know, I'm sure Ituzaingó must be full of mountains. Or maybe it's one of the ones from the Córdoba mountain range who's just decided to take a little walk..."

And I asked again for the paint and the paintbrush, but again he changed the subject and went on asking me questions.

Finally, half an hour later, he lent them to me.

I ran over to where Dailan Kifki was standing.

Everyone was quite baffled when they saw me run past, because they couldn't imagine what I was planning to paint at that hour.

I bet you can't imagine, either.

44

So what did I do?

I painted Dailan Kifki a lovely train passenger outfit!

Would you like me to describe it to you in every last detail?

Well, standing on tiptoes, and occasionally lifted up by the Fireman, I managed to paint Dailan Kifki an enormous polka-dot tie.

I took a few steps back to examine the effect, and saw that it needed a couple more strokes.

But don't for a moment think that I did the painting carelessly and in a slapdash way.

No, sir, I did the painting very carefully and very un-slapdashly indeed.

I painted the lapels of his jacket, first one, then the other.

And then, of course, I drew three very big, very round buttons, just like the Fireman's.

Then, nearly down to his knees (the elephant's knees, not the Fireman's), I painted some jacket pockets.

You'll be wondering now how I drew the trousers?

Very simple: a single vertical, ever-so-straight line right down his legs. I painted the left first, and it came out very nicely.

I began painting the other side, starting from the top. It was coming out as perfectly straight as a ruler, and I was nearly done when... *Ker-BLAM!*

Supisichi!

Something hit me on the head, hard.

I couldn't even cry for help.

I only managed "Hel..."

And I fainted.

The blow to my head was as calamitous as it was unexpected.

All of a sudden I saw seven hundred and eighty-nine little stars and I flopped down onto the platform of Ituzaingó station.

I thought I'd died.

45

N ope.

When I awoke from my faint, everyone was standing around fanning me, slapping me and throwing cold water over me.

Granddad was consulting his First Aid manual.

The Fireman was connecting his hose up to the tap to give me a good drenching.

My Auntie Clodomira was twirling her umbrella, wailing:

"How many more accidents are we going to have to put up with from this pesky elephant?!"

I managed to open one eye. Then I managed to open the other. Then I managed to open my mouth a little.

And then I asked:

"Wh—wha—ha—happ—happened?"

"That nasty, rude, horrible elephant!" said my Auntie Clodomira.

"I won't let you call him such horrible things, Auntie," I said, waking up properly now.

"You ought to know, he was the one who knocked you out with his trunk and nearly killed you," explained my aunt, colouring with rage.

"That's not possible," I said. "It must have been an accident. Dailan Kifki has never hurt anybody, except when he's being attacked."

"No, sir, this is a terrible elephant, an errible, errible telephant," my aunt insisted, jumbling her words in sheer rage and banging on the platform with her umbrella.

I went to find the rest of the retinue to see if someone calmer and more serene might be able to explain the really truthful truth to me.

What ever could have happened?

Well, apparently, while I was starting to paint Dailan Kifki's outfit, the poor thing was fast asleep, with that curious habit he has of sleeping with his trunk up in the air.

And just as I was crouching down to paint the stripe of his trousers, it seems the poor thing had a bad dream and *Ker-BLAM!*... Down fell his trunk.

Naturally, it fell on my head.

Poor Dailan Kifki was looking at me in great distress, as if to say: "I didn't mean it, I didn't mean it, my trunk just fell, I had no idea you were down there."

I finally managed to clear my head, and I saw that my work had all been wasted. Because when Dailan Kifki's trunk was down, it completely covered the necktie and the pretty buttons I'd painted on him.

"Get that trunk back up!" I said as forcefully as I could.

Nothing.

"Lift that trunk up now!"

Nothing.

"Trunk! Up!"

Nothing.

But then my brother Roberto appeared, elbowing his way through the crowds, and he said:

"Leave it to me. I understand about elephants." He approached Dailan Kifki, lifted his ear with some effort and shouted:

"Either-you-hold-your-trunk-up-this-minute-or-there's-no-more-lovely-oats-soup-for-you!"

Then Dailan Kifki did raise his trunk nice and high and finally the necktie and buttons shone.

"Don't you think Dailan Kifki could pass for a train passenger, now he's painted like that?" I asked.

"Of course," everybody replied. "You can hardly tell he's an elephant now."

And I was so pleased with my handiwork that I did a few little folkdancey steps right there on the platform.

46

Would you like me to tell you how we all travelled back from Ituzaingó?

Well, we travelled back, returning home, that is, by train.

Dailan Kifki, with his trunk curled up the whole time and his passenger outfit, settled himself into a seat, with a pretending expression on his face.

Fortunately the compartment was empty, so all the rest of us hurried to fill the remaining seats.

Fortunately the guard was a bit short-sighted and he didn't notice a thing.

Fortunately we all arrived safe and sound at Miserere Square.

From there we walked over to my house, which is all the way up in the neighbourhood of Palermo.

It was pretty tiring, and don't forget that by now our shoes were in a wretched state.

At that time of the morning the streets were practically deserted, so we didn't draw too much attention to ourselves.

Finally we arrived at my house, and everyone who could came in for breakfast.

I took Dailan Kifki out into the garden. He seemed really happy.

I left him there chatting away with the flowers and the ants, and went back into the kitchen to make him a nice barrel of lovely, milky oats soup.

We all had our breakfast, and then the sad moment came for us to say our goodbyes.

The truth was, we had become quite fond of one another, and nobody wanted to go home.

I had to promise them a party very soon, and only then did they start to file out, with tears in their eyes.

The Superintendent, using his truncheon and his white gloves, was able to keep everyone more or less in order.

We were first presented with the farewell greetings of the Ambassadors, then the Mini-Secretary, who had become tinier than ever with all this adventuring.

Then came the Mayor, then the director of the La Plata Astronomical Observatory, then the Admirable Admiral, then the Captain of the Firemen, then the ice-cream sellers, and finally the dog with two tails.

And there was so much weeping from all of them that they made quite an impressive uproar.

At that moment the doorbell rang.

When I opened it, I found a handsome postman the colour of milky coffee.

Ker-BLAM! I thought to myself. He must have come to complain that with all the uproar the stamps have come unstuck again at the post office.

Nope.

The postman took off his cap and asked:

"Is there anyone living here by the name of Dailan Kifki?"

I needn't tell you that all the people who'd already said goodbye just stood there, as they were much too curious to leave now.

"Yes, Mister Dailan Kifki lives here," everyone answered.

"All these letters are for him," said the postman, taking three million envelopes out of his bag.

I took the envelopes in my arms and ran out to the garden, followed by the whole retinue, which now included the postman, to read them to Dailan Kifki.

Very nervously I opened the first.

It was from the Director of the zoo, and it said something like:

"The Director of the Zoological Gardens invites you and your family to the grand bazaar and party in honour of Dailan Kifki, the first flying elephant in the whole republic."

Can you imagine anything more exciting?

The next letter was from the aviators' club, who wanted to give Dailan Kifki a medal.

Another was from an ambassador, who wanted to bestow some honour or other on him.

Another was from the Astronautical Phantasmagorical University of Calamuchita, who wanted to name him Doctor Honoris Causa.

And so many more like them.

Letters from everyone!

It took me, like, three hours to read them all.

When I'd finished, I could see that Dailan Kifki was moved, and he had big thick tears running down his trunk.

Everybody was hugging one another and crying. They decided to head home for a change of clothes and come back tomorrow to go to the big party at the zoo.

When I had finished saying goodbye to everyone, I closed the door and was alone at last.

I was just about to take a little nap when...

The doorbell rang:

Ring,
      ring,
            ring.

Who could it be?

47

I opened the door to see an impressive-looking gentleman with very black skin standing outside.

I could tell at once that he was a king, because he had a lovely gold crown on his head, with little pearls and diamonds.

He was wearing a richly coloured shirt all embroidered in silver and gold, covered in decorations and tassels and trinkets.

Behind him was a train of fourteen people who had just got out of six golden cars.

Ker-BLAM! I bet it's King Balthasar! I thought, suddenly remembering it was nearly Christmas.

I invited the King and his guests inside.

My whole family watched with their mouths open.

You can't imagine how embarrassed I was not to have a single chair to offer such an important visitor!

And how embarrassed I was that he should see my house looking so dirty and topsy-turvy.

I invited him to sit on the floor, and we all joined him down there to talk.

The King opened his mouth and said something like:

"Bayumba bombé tangolé golé golé."

I was all ready to send Roberto off to buy a dictionary, when one of his people, the interpreter, explained the whole thing to me.

This man was indeed a king, but not King Balthasar. He was the King of a distant African kingdom called Ugambalanda.

But besides being a king, do you know who else he was?

He was the owner of Dailan Kifki's mother!

It turned out that newspapers all over the world had printed stories about the extraordinary feats carried out by my elephant, which was how Mister King had learnt about him, and putting two and two together, he'd come to the conclusion that Dailan Kifki was the son of a famous elephant he had in his African palace.

And it turned out that once upon a time, a hunter had stolen the baby elephant away from his mother and sold him to the owner of a circus, who brought him here to Argentina.

The circus owner had gone broke, closed the circus and abandoned poor Dailan Kifki, who, as you will remember, showed up one morning at my front door.

"And his mum?" I asked King Pochoclo (because that's what His Majesty was called).

"His mum is not far away," said the King, "and tomorrow she'll be coming to the party at the zoo to be reunited with her baby."

Once he had finished saying this, King Pochoclo and his whole retinue got up and said goodbye till the following day.

And once again, I was completely astonished.

48

The following day—that glorious day of great public tributes to Dailan Kifki—we were awoken by a volley of cannon-fire.

I got up and ran to the garden to give my elephant a bath. King Pochoclo had sent a gift: some opulent apparel for Dailan Kifki to wear on this very grand occasion.

A saddle of golden velvet, braids and tassels for his head and ears, and an honorary astronaut's helmet.

Roberto helped me bathe Dailan Kifki before saddling him up so luxuriously.

Then we all put on our finery and walked out the front door to where our retinue of the previous days was waiting for us. They were all so dolled up we hardly recognised them!

Granddad had put on—and I honestly have no idea which museum he'd got it from—a lovely uniform of a Patrician Guard.

My Auntie Clodomira was dressed in sky-blue organdie.

My dad had a new poncho.

I don't even have to tell you that the numbers of TV cameramen, journalists, photographers, busybodies and ice-cream sellers had multiplied a million times.

Since the zoo isn't too far from my house, we all went on foot. Dailan Kifki led the parade.

We all walked very slowly, in time with the Boy Scouts' band, who played a slow, stately march.

At the zoo we were met by the most senior officials and King Pochoclo with his whole retinue.

But there was one thing I couldn't stop wondering about, and I was already getting emotional just thinking about it: what would it be like when Dailan Kifki met his mother?

Because we hadn't told him a thing.

And what if King Pochoclo was wrong and it turned out that his elephant wasn't Dailan Kifki's mother after all?

But I supposed he wouldn't have taken such a long journey if he hadn't been completely sure that she was.

Finally we entered the zoo, which was decorated with flags from every country.

There was another volley of cannon-fire, applause, cheers, shouts, a few faintings and a shower of confetti and streamers.

Still moving in time with the Boy Scouts' band, we made our way solemnly towards the official stage, beside which stood— looking very serious and decked out with a gold saddle—Dailan Kifki's mother.

When Dailan Kifki saw her, he forgot all about the retinue, the party, the solemnity and the order we'd managed to keep up to that moment.

As though he'd been pricked with a knitting needle, he tore off towards the stage where he embraced his mother, snorting with excitement.

The two of them stood with their trunks wrapped around each other's necks for nearly an hour. They whispered and puffed away to each other, lifting their ears as a sign of happiness.

Then the speeches started, which naturally I shan't transcribe so as not to bore you. And finally we all were served hot chocolate with croissants, right in front of the monkey cage.

I don't need to tell you the day had been declared a national holiday.

Once the ceremony was over, we decided it was time for us all to go back to our respective homes, but now a real puzzle presented itself.

Nobody had thought about it, nobody had a clever, practical solution for such a terrible problem.

We couldn't separate Dailan Kifki from his mother, could we?

Nor could I be separated from Dailan Kifki, because I'd become so attached to him, right?

So that was the problem: where on earth were the two elephants going to live?

Even just one could barely fit in my garden.

We began to discuss the problem.

The Director of the zoo, very obligingly, offered to house them in his distinguished institution.

King Pochoclo offered to take them back to Ugambalanda.

Granddad offered to take care of them in his house in Ituzaingó.

But I didn't want to be separated from them.

When I was just about ready to start crying at the hopelessness of the whole situation, someone put his hand on my shoulder and said sweetly that I needn't worry, that we were going to live together and everything would come up roses, we'd eat partridges for dinner and we'd also blow our noses.

It was the Fireman.

And right there, quite unexpectedly, he asked me to marry him, and he said we could go and live on his aunt and uncle's farm, where there was more than enough space for two well-behaved elephants.

I was dumbstruck again, and slowly looked at everybody, one by one, as though asking their advice.

Everyone had fallen impressively silent, and they were all looking down at their newly shined shoes.

Then, hesitant and shy, I looked at the Fireman, and once again I saw what a good fellow he was, and how brave, and kind, and affectionate, and sweet-smelling, and, above all, how much he loved elephants.

I told him I'd think about it.

Everyone gave a sigh of relief.

Mister First Officer of the Capital Fire Brigade, Don Agapito Campolongo, has the pleasure of inviting you and your family to his wedding, which will take place very early next Wednesday morning. The bride and groom will make their way to the ceremony riding on the back of Dailan Kifki, and from their positions up on top they will greet their guests and offer them magnificent hot chocolate in pretty little porcelain cups.

The bride and groom would also like to invite their guests to accompany them to the port of the city, from where they will be departing, together with their two elephants, for the Kingdom of Ugambalanda on their honeymoon.

Photographs of Dailan Kifki and his mother will be distributed free to members of the public, and commemorative pennants will be donated by Mister Don Carozo Minujin.

Translator's Note

This book was translated at The Banff Centre in June 2015, under the auspices of BILTC, the Banff International Literary Translation Centre. The translator is enormously grateful to all the programme's staff for the warm welcome, the hospitality, the food and the views; and to director Katie Silver and his fellow participants for three unimprovable weeks packed with all the myriad delights of their company. Translators don't typically get to dedicate their books, but if we did, this one would be for them.

PUSHKIN CHILDREN'S BOOKS

We created Pushkin Children's Books to share tales from different languages and cultures with younger readers, and to open the door to the wide, colourful worlds these stories offer.

From picture books and adventure stories to fairy tales and classics, and from fifty-year-old bestsellers to current huge successes abroad, the books on the Pushkin Children's list reflect the very best stories from around the world, for our most discerning readers of all: children.

THE RED ABBEY CHRONICLES: MARESI
MARIA TURTSCHANINOFF

'Stands out for its startling originality, and for the frightening
plausibility of the dangerous world it creates'
Telegraph

THE LETTER FOR THE KING
TONKE DRAGT

'*The Letter for the King* will get pulses racing... Pushkin
Press deserves every praise for publishing this beautifully
translated, well-presented and captivating book'
The Times

THE SECRETS OF THE WILD WOOD
TONKE DRAGT

'Offers intrigue, action and escapism'
Sunday Times

THE PARENT TRAP · THE FLYING CLASSROOM · DOT AND ANTON
ERICH KÄSTNER

Illustrated by Walter Trier

'The bold line drawings by Walter Trier are the work of
genius... As for the stories, if you're a fan of *Emil and the
Detectives*, then you'll find these just as spirited'
Spectator

FROM THE MIXED-UP FILES OF MRS. BASIL E. FRANKWEILER
E. L. KONIGSBURG

'Delightful... I love this book... a beautifully written
adventure, with endearing characters and full of dry
wit, imagination and inspirational confidence'
Daily Mail

THE WILDWITCH SERIES

LENE KAABERBØL

1 · *Wildfire*
2 · *Oblivion*
3 · *Life Stealer*
4 · *Bloodling*

'Classic fantasy adventure... Young readers will be delighted to
hear that there are more adventures to come for Clara'
Lovereading

MEET AT THE ARK AT EIGHT!

ULRICH HUB

Illustrated by Jörg Mühle

'Of all the books about a penguin in a suitcase pretending to be God
asking for a cheesecake, this one is absolutely, definitely my favourite'
Independent

THE SNOW QUEEN

HANS CHRISTIAN ANDERSEN

Illustrated by Lucie Arnoux

'A lovely edition [of a] timeless story'
The Lady

IN THEIR SHOES: FAIRY TALES AND FOLKTALES

Illustrated by Lucie Arnoux

'An eclectic, shoe-themed collection... arrestingly illustrated by Lucie Arnoux'
Sunday Times

THE CAT WHO CAME IN OFF THE ROOF

ANNIE M.G. SCHMIDT

'Guaranteed to make anyone 7-plus to 107 who likes to
curl up with a book and a cat purr with pleasure'
The Times

LAFCADIO: THE LION WHO SHOT BACK
SHEL SILVERSTEIN

'A story which is really funny, yet also teaches us a great deal about what we want, what we think we want and what we are no longer certain about once we have it'
Irish Times

THE PILOT AND THE LITTLE PRINCE
PETER SÍS

'With its extraordinary, sophisticated illustrations, its poetry and the historical detail of the text, this book will reward readers of any age over eight'
Sunday Times

THE STORY OF THE BLUE PLANET
ANDRI SNÆR MAGNASON
Illustrated by Áslaug Jónsdóttir

'A Seussian mix of wonder, wit and gravitas'
The New York Times

THE WITCH IN THE BROOM CUPBOARD AND OTHER TALES
PIERRE GRIPARI
Illustrated by Fernando Puig Rosado

'Wonderful... funny, tender and daft'
David Almond

THE WHALE THAT FELL IN LOVE WITH A SUBMARINE
AKIYUKI NOSAKA
Illustrated by Mika Provata-Carlone

'Remarkable stories... They are dark but so beautiful, so profound; subtle and elegant. It is a book that will last all your life'
Irish Times

SHOLA AND THE LIONS

BERNARDO ATXAGA

Illustrated by Mikel Valverde

'Gently ironic stories... totally charming'
Independent

THE POINTLESS LEOPARD: WHAT GOOD ARE KIDS ANYWAY?

COLAS GUTMAN

Illustrated by Delphine Perret

'Lively, idiomatic and always entertaining... a decidedly offbeat little book'
Robert Dunbar, *Irish Times*

POCKETY: THE TORTOISE WHO LIVED AS SHE PLEASED

FLORENCE SEYVOS

Illustrated by Claude Ponti

'A treasure – a real find – and one of the most enjoyable children's books I've read in a while... This is a tortoise that deserves to win every literary race'
Observer

SAVE THE STORY

GULLIVER · ANTIGONE · CAPTAIN NEMO · DON JUAN
GILGAMESH · THE BETROTHED · THE NOSE
CYRANO DE BERGERAC · KING LEAR · CRIME AND PUNISHMENT

'An amazing new series from Pushkin Press in which literary, adult authors retell classics (with terrific illustrations) for a younger generation'
Daily Telegraph

THE OKSA POLLOCK SERIES

ANNE PLICHOTA AND CENDRINE WOLF

1 · *The Last Hope*
2 · *The Forest of Lost Souls*
3 · *The Heart of Two Worlds*
4 · *Tainted Bonds*

'A feisty heroine, lots of sparky tricks and evil opponents could fill a gap left by the end of the Harry Potter series'
Daily Mail